SING TO ME

Shonagh Koea is a fulltime writer who lives and works in Auckland. Her first short story collection, *The Woman Who Never Went Home*, was published in 1987 and her first novel, *The Grandiflora Tree*, in 1989. Her second novel, *Staying Home and Being Rotten*, was published in 1992 and received outstanding acclaim. It was followed by another collection of short stories, *Fifteen Rubies By Candlelight*, in 1993. Her short stories have appeared in magazines, mainly the *Listener*, since 1981 when she won the Air New Zealand Short Story Award. The QE II Arts Council's Literature Programme awarded her the Additional Writing Bursary in 1989 and a second Writing Bursary in 1992. In 1993 she was Literary Fellow at the University of Auckland where *Sing to Me, Dreamer* was written.

OTHER BOOKS BY THE SAME AUTHOR

The Woman Who Never Went Home
The Grandiflora Tree
Staying Home and Being Rotten
Fifteen Rubies by Candlelight

Shonagh Koea

SING TO ME, DREAMER

𝒱

VINTAGE

The author wishes to thank the University of
Auckland for awarding her their Literary Fellowship
in 1993, which enabled her to write this novel.

Vintage New Zealand
Random House New Zealand Ltd
(An imprint of the Random House Group)

18 Poland Road
Glenfield
Auckland 10
NEW ZEALAND

Associated companies, branches and representatives
throughout the world.

First published 1994
© Shonagh Koea 1994
Reprinted 1994
ISBN 1 86941 233 8
Printed in Malaysia

CHAPTER ONE

"IF YOU MADE some attempt to fit in," says Goldblatt, "people might ask you out." He sits back in his very expensive office chair of chromium and navy-blue hide and crosses his legs. His thighs are blubbery but Goldblatt swings his left leg over the right with the ease of long practice. Vaguely, I recall Goldblatt when we were all at school together years ago, and he was a fat boy even then.

"If you made some attempt to talk to people," he says, "if you struck up a conversation with someone you might make friends. People might make themselves known to you. But," says Goldblatt, "you always were standoffish, now weren't you?" Goldblatt obviously remembers everything as well as I do. The fat boy, the unpopular girl who read books and spent most of her time in the library. The obese lawyer, the lady in the yellow silk sari. We are not much changed. Only the clothes are different.

"What will I talk about?"

I am sitting as far away from Goldblatt as possible, my seat by the windows giving me an unparalleled view of the street below. We are three floors up in Goldblatt's own building, the lower levels let to real estate agents, with a takeaway bar round the back. Every inch is utilised to earn. Goldblatt's father put the building up long before I went to university and he used liver-coloured brick which has aged remarkably well. Goldblatt's father was a butcher with a canny eye on the offal and a taste for small windows. Goldblatt looks like him except that he has a wider vocabulary and better clothes. I sit there wondering if I look like my late mother and have a

1

wider international vocabulary — I speak Hindi and fluent French which Goldblatt probably resents — and I wear peculiar clothes, by Goldblatt's standards. My mother was a great one for the well-cut suit in all seasons, with a brooch at the lapel. Linen or silk in the summer; pure wool in winter, the odd little cashmere jersey. That was Mother. I wear saris, or Indian trousers in muslin with tunics over the top.

"Perhaps the weather," says Goldblatt, "but stay off politics. And religion. Stay right off religion. And for God's sake," he says with fascinating irony, "I do implore you, Margaret, don't ever tell a soul you're a Hindu. I must say," says Goldblatt, "and I feel I must tell you this frankly and categorically, I never told your mother you'd become a Hindu. That is one thing I never passed on."

My communication with my family for the past twenty years has been solely through Goldblatt, the family lawyer, in taciturn annual exchanges. *Your father has had an operation for cancer of the prostate. Your father has been diagnosed as being terminally ill. Your father has died.* These constitute the messages for three years. *Your sister Sylvia has married an accountant whom we like very much. Your sister Sylvia has given birth to stillborn twins. Your sister Sylvia has died suddenly and tragically of kidney failure.* Another three years. *Your mother is suffering from Alzheimer's disease. Your mother has died.* Ranji did not bother to send many messages on my account.

I know he sent one the second year I lived in the north of India. *Regret to inform you that your daughter Margaret has suffered a severe breakdown but is progressing well with the help of a holy man I have brought from Agra.* I don't think that one would have gone down well. There were one or two others over the years. *In answer to your enquiry, no I have not married your daughter Margaret but do be assured that at all times she is treated with honour and generosity.* Goldblatt used to relay these messages back and forth.

"Just steer very well clear of anything about Hindus," says Goldblatt. "Talk about tennis. Weren't you the one who was a very good tennis player?"

"That was Sylvia."

"You make everything so difficult, Margaret. If I may say so, you seem to take a fiendish delight in making everything as difficult as possible. Even if you weren't a tennis player it surely wouldn't be too difficult to talk about tennis, would it?" Goldblatt leans forward and puts his head in his hands. I can imagine we must have been a difficult family to deal with over the years.

"And there's also the question of clothes, Margaret." He coughs and I wonder if we have choked Goldblatt with our antics for more than two decades. "Clothes." He speaks like the son of a butcher, the atmosphere heavy with reproach, meaty with old blame and disgrace. It was Goldblatt who had to tell my mother I had been taken to Wellington Hospital by ambulance after my collapse in front of the main entrance to Kirkcaldie and Stains. He must have been just out of law school then, a green young lawyer anxious to please but with a sad and difficult message to deliver.

Goldblatt's face is impassive. He looks like a man suffering from controllable melancholia. My yellow silk sari is fluttering round my ankles in the breeze from the windows. From far below comes the sound of music. 'Greensleeves' is being played through a loudspeaker from an ice-cream truck brightly painted as a wagon for a festival, brilliant as the light from a hundred candles lit for Diwali. When Goldblatt and I went to school in this town we bought ice-creams at the corner shop and I would like to ask somebody now what happened to the corner shops and why are ice-creams sold from vans painted in luminous pastel colours.

"If you have any questions," says Goldblatt, "you'd be most welcome to ask. I sometimes wonder" — and he looks at me like a merchant assessing currency — "exactly what does go on in your head. My mother used to say, God bless her, that it's the quiet ones you have to watch." If I ask Goldblatt about ice-creams at this juncture is he likely to interpret the question as a manifestation of cretinism, the secretive greediness of the very sly?

"I seem to have given you food for thought there." Goldblatt is pleased with himself. "I'll leave the ball in your court on that, and you can come back to me anytime. And now — to get back to the business of clothes, Margaret. Clothes. The signals by which we state our aims and desires, our place in the greater scheme of things. Clothes, Margaret."

Apart from my yellow sari, I am wearing a gauzy silk jacket sewn with thin golden medallions — my banking system on my back, if only Goldblatt knew it, and I have also put a large diamond brooch on my left shoulder to hold a flutter of chiffon. If Goldblatt is right about the message clothing gives to the world, then my message is very plain. I want to go back to India and I do not trust banks. The brooch is very old and the stones are quite dull. They are of Georgian cut, important only to a connoisseur, and the whole article was made long ago *en tremblant* by a craftsman who favoured that mode so it would be recognised only by an expert. My banking is always discreet.

"If you looked — well, you know what I mean, Margaret. You were always quite a bright girl at school, if I remember correctly. You could find something in your mother's wardrobe, a nice suit or dress or something." He waves one arm in the air and makes a hasty sketch of something severe and tailored. "And if you just chatted away to people about the weather and sport and a few normal things like that, well, I feel sure" — and he stops there; perhaps all Goldblatt feels absolutely sure about is his growing uncertainty. "Well, all I can say is that I feel a great certainty that people would come forward, Margaret. People would come forward."

"Do you do a lot of court work?" I ask. It has come to me, sitting there, that there is something courtly about his repetitions, about his rhetoric. I can almost hear Goldblatt defending me. *And I ask you, members of the jury, is this woman's crime simply one of wearing the wrong clothes, and at the wrong time?*

"Margaret, we're talking about your clothes today, and your mother's estate. Some other time, when we have a few more minutes at our disposal, I'll answer any questions you may like to throw at me about my career. But in the meantime, I'd advise you to find something, you know, more ordinary in one of the wardrobes. And I can tell you for a fact that there are one or two girls who went to school with you who might very well wish to renew old friendships. Just stick to the weather, stay off politics and religion, don't mention Hinduism and you'll be amazed. Thank you, Daphne," he calls over my shoulder, and when I look around, one of the

4

girls has come in from the outer office, noiseless in Gucci loafers.

"In a minute, when Miss Harris has gone." So I have to go, do I. Already I am rising to my feet. My own shoes are yellow satin ballet slippers sewn with cabochon rubies, a lower grade of stone but still possessing some value. More of my banking. The girl in the Gucci loafers looks at me without respect. My clothing signals do not fit in with her sartorial vocabulary. I am probably the wife of a fruiterer accused of theft or in trouble with the Inland Revenue Department over shipments of rotten bananas.

"And with cream today, Daphne. Two spoons of brown sugar. And I'll have a bagel."

The breeze from the door as it closes behind Daphne and her loafers makes the golden discs on my jacket tremble. When I have left, they are all going to tuck in to a merry little afternoon tea and I will have to walk back to my mother's house considering all these topics of conversation that Goldblatt says will make me more presentable. But will I, thus, be more presentable, even wearing one of my mother's suits, and will I be able to manage these topics when all I've talked about for years is maharaja's gossip. And I have talked about politics. I have gossiped about politics. I remember when Gayatri Devi was jailed by Indira Gandhi. I remember before that, when she went on her political campaigns through the Indian villages and the women were spellbound, as much by her beauty as her oratory. I have a picture of her in a sari of jasmine-coloured silk, sitting on an embroidered cloth with a glass of water in one languid and beautiful hand while around her hundreds of women squat, heads bowed, awaiting her words. Am I now to speak of all that to round-faced complacent women with whom I once played basket-ball when we were all hardly more than children?

I used to lie on my golden cushions with my arms wrapped around Ranji's neck and he would whisper all these stories in my ear, all these stories that did the rounds of the other royal households, including the latest one. The latest one, then, was the biggest and best of them all but, in time, it became an old story. After more time passed it became an almost forgotten story and it is the strands of this tale that I wind about myself in invisible and comforting filaments as I climb the hill to my mother's house after yet another weekly meeting with Goldblatt.

There was once a maharaja, the story goes, who loved cricket and accompanied an Indian cricket team on a tour of Australasia. In an obscure seaside city he gathered up a golden-haired mistress to bring home with him. She was a great intellectual who knew Dickens backwards, and in her house of rose-coloured stone in an Indian city far to the north she recited Shakespeare and Keats and Byron and blinded him for other women. I did not have — do not have — an incomplete doctorate in literature for nothing. Am I to chatter to people about all that? Shall I tell them that the Maharaja of Patiala liked a virgin a day but in old age cut down to one a week. I could tell them that the Maharaja of Kapurthala's favourite wife was an English girl called Stella Mudge, and when I went to London I would sometimes have afternoon tea with Stella at Brown's Hotel in Belgravia because we had a lot in common, including fine long legs, but Stella was married and I was not and, in the fullness of time, that makes a difference.

"Just stick to the weather," Goldblatt had said, "and you can't go wrong, and if I might make just one more tiny suggestion, may I most respectfully suggest that hereabouts we do not wear diamante jewellery in the daytime." Goldblatt's face is as round as a pie. "It's just considered a tiny bit cheap, Margaret, just a tiny bit cheap, but you weren't to know. Don't let it upset you. It's just a very small point for you to ponder at your leisure."

I place one hand over my diamond brooch. It is a very old brooch and the stones have a Georgian cut that makes them dull and watery. It also makes them curiously valuable because of rarity and age. When I get to London again, if I ever get to London, I will sell the brooch at Sotheby's by auction or at one of the big jewellers like Wartski or Collingwood. Any of them would do, it just depends where I would get the best price and I will decide that when the time comes.

"If you just" — and Goldblatt hesitates here — "kind of moderated things a bit, Margaret. If you didn't make such a display of yourself all the time." I look through an inner window in Goldblatt's office and two typists are staring at me. "You might find you'd get along a whole lot better. We just have to wait this one out, Margaret, and you might as well do so in comfort with a little company. I mean, for instance, why don't you consider buying some kind of little car to get about in rather than tramp everywhere in that get-up." He flaps a hand towards my chiffon and diamonds. "I don't mean anything as full scale as my own Mercedes, of course." His laughter is deprecating, but delighted. "Perhaps a little Honda might do. That's what I mean, Margaret, by making yourself a bit comfortable and then you might meet a few people and make friends. You could go out and about for little drives. It could be quite good fun for you."

He is right, of course. Such people often are. That is what they are paid for. We are waiting for probate to be granted my mother's will. I am the sole beneficiary simply because I am the last one left. There is no one else left alive in the family. If my mother had liked cats, which she did not, she may have left everything to the cats' home. If she liked dogs, ditto. If she had cared about the homeless, Methodists, Presbyterians, Roman Catholics, the unemployed, orphans, unmarried mothers or, indeed, anybody, she would have left the estate to them. But there is only me left so it was left to me and I now have these weekly meetings with Goldblatt to see how things are going.

"Anyway, till next week," said Goldblatt. He is standing and my weekly appointment is over. His bagel and coffee with cream awaits. "Sorry I haven't any news for you, but sometimes they're very slow. Wheels within wheels, my dear, wheels within wheels. But in the meantime, do give some thought to what I've said and I hope I haven't offended you by mentioning the bit of tinsel."

He points to the brooch again and lifts a fat red hand in salutation as I go down the stairs to the street. Outside, the town of Hillingdon lies spread before me. Goldblatt's offices are on the highest point for miles. Seven blocks away is my mother's house, packed from floor to ceiling in almost every room with crates and suitcases into which she squeezed all

7

clothing, memorabilia, small furniture, china, anything she could lay her hands on in the place. My mother, during her last bewildered years, has meticulously packed up her entire life and it is now my task to unpack it all, to prepare it for auction.

"Margaret?" It is Goldblatt's voice again. He has followed me down the stairs and is calling across the pavement to me now. "Margaret, someone told me the most extraordinary thing today. Somebody told me that you had an elephant at your place, that there's an elephant tethered in your back-yard. I said, 'Well I feel very sure that it's just some silly story someone's made up. Perhaps someone saw the shadow of the chimney or the shape of a tree against a shed or something. You get these old people,' I said, 'and they can't see an inch in front of their own noses, let alone anyone else's, and they see all sorts of silly things as darkness falls on yet another day of boredom. I'll ask her myself,' I said, 'because she's coming in today to see me about the estate. I'll have a little chat to her and solve the mystery.'"

"It's true." The light from the sun has caught that from my diamond brooch and I see its watery glitter reflected in a puddle. In Hillingdon you seldom get a day without rain.

Goldblatt is coming across the pavement now and he is followed by Daphne, the girl in Gucci loafers. She is carrying a cup and saucer in one hand and has a plate in the other.

"Not now, Daphne. Later, Daphne. Later. I said I'd have it later, when Miss Harris has gone and Miss Harris" — he gestures towards me with that fat hand again — "has not yet gone, Daphne. Just put the saucer over the cup to keep it hot and I'll be back in a minute." The figure of a wilted Daphne disappears behind the swing doors.

"It's true that there's an elephant in my garden. Whoever told you about him being tied up at the back of the house was telling the absolute truth," I say. It is a strange feeling, standing on the pavement being questioned by Goldblatt. It is almost like being on trial in an impromptu court. "But I can explain. There's a very logical explanation and it isn't as silly as you might think, or as difficult either. In a funny way, it isn't unlike having a dog, a big one like, say, an Airedale or a —" I get no further than this.

8

"Margaret." Goldblatt is shaking his head, sad as a deflated Easter bunny. There is something very comfortable, very marshmallowy, even chocolatey, about his middle. "Oh, Margaret. Margaret, Margaret, Margaret." His voice is fading now. He has followed the girl through the swing doors for the restorative coffee, with cream and a bagel.

"But it isn't fair," I shout after him, such a big voice I hardly recognise it as my own. I have become apologetic in recent times. Terrified. Silenced. Netta would hardly recognise me now, Netta who looked after me in my pink stone house and seemed like my sister.

"It was you who got your Godamn brother to send me a guard dog, only it wasn't a guard dog at all, it was a bloody elephant. If it's anyone's fault, it's yours, Goldblatt." I am becoming a bold and abusive woman. But Goldblatt has gone and all I can hear is the noise of the swing doors, flick-flack flick-flack, as they close after him. Goldblatt, procurer of elephants for sari-clad women of doubtful provenance, has gone. I set off, between showers, to my mother's house and as I go I reflect upon the words of the holy man whom Ranji brought from Agra to talk to me so long ago. The holy man said that all happiness is the flower of duty. Why, then, was I most happy when I was not dutiful and why am I so unhappy now that I have dutifully come home to administer my mother's estate? Why is that?

At my mother's house, the sun in the late afternoon comes to the rooms through one unobscured window on the upstairs landing where I sleep. The upstairs landing has become my bedroom because it is the only area that is now reasonably clean and free of rubbish and packing cases. All the other casements upstairs are covered with crates and boxes though I have made inroads into them, the task seemingly futile because I unpack merely to pack again. But I repack with care and discernment, taste and an eye to value, and I have lists to prove it, lengthy résumés of possessions which have been sent already to various auction houses to be sold. Whether this is legal or not I do not know. Probate has not yet been granted my mother's will but I am the sole beneficiary and I have to keep myself occupied profitably somehow. It seems best and more discreet to keep my mother's small shames private. The whole town would cackle if it became known that she packed up the garbage with her wedding dress and the underwear she was married in — she was always an absurdly sentimental woman — and that old potato peelings had atrophied on the crutch of her bridal knickers. If Goldblatt knew what I was doing I feel certain he might debate it.

But now, as I step in the front door, a light film of dust motes stirs and my own packing greets me, my ranks of repacked boxes that lead through the entrance hall and into the kitchen, each one clearly labelled. *Clothes of the 1920s. Clothes of the 1930s. Hats (winter) from the 1940s. Hats (summer) from the 1940s. Six Armand Marseilles dolls. A selection of early costume jewellery. Books: royal reminiscences.* The selection is quaint and ridiculous and viewed in the faint golden light of that faded afternoon it has a foolish chic that touches my lack of heart in a trifling way. It has the effect of piano music heard across a river, rising and fading with the noise of the water. High in the sky a flock of seabirds cries across the bay and I think for a moment the sound comes from a baby keening, a lost baby who always haunts me in the calls of birds, the scraping of dry branches on windows, all the cadences of the world, and the most haunting thing about the sound is that my second emotion is always a kind of gentle fear. I have no experience with children and would not know how to look after a baby if I found one.

In the sitting room, the sunset glows through red velvet curtains that have faded to the colour of old roses and it illuminates the march-past of souvenirs across the mantelpiece. Various items in the cases and trunks have caught my fancy so they are in a row on the old shelf above the fireplace. They are beautiful and they look as if they are meant to be there, that they have been placed in those exact positions by design. There is a Chinese cylinder vase on a rosewood stand and beside it sits a wooden moneybox shaped like a pear and probably carved from pearwood. I have looked inside it and it is full of Australian $50 notes, all neatly folded in four and wound tightly together so they are like the interior of a banking snail. A Wedgwood jug in deepest indigo is next, with grape garlands and mythical figures of women in a landscape. Perhaps they are the concubines of rulers, henchwomen of monarchs, precursors of myself and my journey so long ago from this house and everything it meant.

"Next year I may be able to afford a tennis court," my father said one morning at breakfast, a week before I ran away from home in a stolen car. There is no tennis court here, no sign of anything like that amidst the rank grass and fallen fences. He must have given up the idea of his garden being a sporting venue after I went away and my sister Sylvia married the accountant they liked so very much. I have found no sign of him in the unpacking. I have found my sister's toys and her wedding dress, but no underwear with potato peelings engrimed.

Of the desirable accountant there remains no sign, not even a wedding photograph. He has been expunged, just as I have, but, of the two of us, his crime would have been the lesser. He married and impregnated my sister and subsequently she and her children died. It was probably just bad luck. Perhaps he married someone else later. He may, at this moment, be laughing in a brightly lit kitchen with a second wife to whom he has been espoused for twenty years, another set of twins playing in the backyard. There were no twins in our family so perhaps he was a man who fathered in multiples. If I had discovered any photographs amongst the mess I have dealt with so far I might have put them on the mantelpiece out of curiosity, so I could better study the lost and mouldering civilisation spawned and spurned in this house. There have been none. Mother seems to have been almost intoxicated by possessions but the owners attract little attention from her.

On a tiny bronze easel at the other end of the mantelpiece I have placed my used air tickets with that unaccustomed name I had not heard for two decades. Miss Margaret Harris, passenger from New Delhi to Singapore, Sydney, Auckland, Hillingdon. And the vouchers are all sadly torn out, the taxi chits used, the hotel bookings for nights of melancholy lodging ripped from their moorings. It was a journey not can-

11

celled, so I am here looking at Mother's mantelpiece. I did not escape my homecoming.

A small silver box with a shard of Ming porcelain mounted on the lid jostles with a gold watch made by Jaeger-le-Coultre that I once took from the old palace treasury. "Choose something. Take something, my sweetheart," Ranji said, so I stretched out my idle hand and took the golden disc as a child might take a big penny. It is part of my portable and secret banking system and awaits sale at a suitable moment. The case is 18-carat and the hallmark shows a rare date so I may do well. The only photograph on the mantelpiece is one of myself, taken at the Taj Mahal about ten years ago. In it I am turning slightly towards the camera, yet my eyes are fixed on some distant sight, another horizon not yet caught on celluloid, and I placed this picture behind the Ming-lidded box yesterday like the last small signal of a long journey. The assembly of little things I have put in that unarranged row are like my own small hand prints as I crawl towards some conclusion of this appalling mess. Inside the house the smell of dead mice is lessening. My cleaning and scrubbing and disinfecting is taking effect. The blue poison pellets the man in the garden shop sold me have taken effect also and the faint scrabblings and nibblings and the running of tiny feet have ceased.

Outside, the elephant grazes quietly at the back of the house. He has eaten all the apples off the very top of the old tree where once my sister and I had a swing and he is contemplating a row of gerberas. Like the myth of the baby's cry I also hear the sound of old laughter as my sister and I play in the garden when it was tidy, manicured, and all the roses were newly planted. It is a long time ago and we are wearing blue dresses with smocking on the front — hers is navy, mine is pale. Her dark hair is cut short and mine is in plaits. We are similar, but opposite. And we are on the swing, Sylvia is sitting on the seat and I am standing behind her, working it with my bent knees.

"Higher, higher." We are shouting and laughing and the swing suddenly flips over the branch and we have gone full circle.

CHAPTER TWO

IF YOU DRIVE into Hillingdon by the northern road, the one that goes along the coast, turn left at the clock tower by the library and you will soon get to the house where I lived with the elephant. The Arsehole's house (I never knew his real name) will not be so visible. It is well below the crown of the road, behind my mother's place, and is masked by a belt of rough trees, lawsonianas past their prime but useful as a windbreak. A deathly wind used to hit that area from the eastern part of town, and a valley nearby acted as a funnel for it. The blasts were lethal but all the trees may be gone now. The Arsehole had this phobia about cutting trees down and it is upon this destruction that my whole story pivots. Had it not been for the tree-felling I may have gone back to live in my mother's house for a few months and then I may have gone to London and eked out some sort of existence in a garden flat in Belsize Park or something very high up and with a tiny terrace in Muswell Hill. Sensibly invested in unit trusts of the safest and most basic sort, I would have had sufficient income to go to the supermarket for the odd sardine, three slices of streaky bacon and a sticky bun once or twice a week. My Swiss bank account, equally sensibly managed, would have given me annual holidays in Brighton in small hotels, not actually on the seafront but within walking distance of it, and dinners alone in tiny restaurants off the main drag. I would have had, equally sensibly, the absolute security of thought that this state of affairs would continue till I died naturally or jumped under a bus, depending on whether acceptance took ascendancy over despair or vice versa. The dia-

13

mond brooches, of which the one *en tremblant* is the smallest, would have kept me in warm overcoats, taxis and various treats that make life worth living. This is a slight exaggeration, but I hope you get the picture. That is how it would have been, but for The Arsehole and his tree-felling.

His house had two entrances from two separate streets. One was a right-of-way, narrow and pitted, off my own road. There was another more official way into his property from a back street. There he had a big wooden letterbox and a concrete drive, running down a steep slope, as narrow as a strangled neck. He had no gates. I sometimes wonder now if he marauded out that way too, undeterred by barriers of any kind that he acknowledged. Certainly he had none of his own. But this is conjecture on my part. I spent many months in that house of my mother's all alone, except for the elephant, and it came to be a habit to indulge in these inward dialogues, these thoughtful mastications of events, so a pattern could be established for my own information and satisfaction. I wished — I wish — to understand and it was my own understanding of greed and venery and then my own vigilance that saved me at my mother's house, first from The Arsehole and then from Goldblatt.

When my mother was alive there was no trouble from The Arsehole, or none that I ever heard about from Goldblatt, and he used to be quite talkative sometimes during our weekly appointments. Once he told me about Gloria Thorpy who was a very tall girl in my class at high school. She had long legs and a haughty expression even then.

"Have you ever heard the interesting story about Gloria Thorpy that was," he said. "She's tied the knot two or three times since then but she always keeps her old name. Just pop a wee signature here, if you would?" And he handed me a piece of paper, keeping most of it obscured with his own fingers. "With regard to La Thorpy, thereby hangs a tale, if I may coin a phrase, Margaret. Just along the bottom if you wouldn't mind, and initial the next page, there's a good girl."

"I can't," I said. Goldblatt looked stunned.

"But you have to."

14

"No, I don't," I said. "And I can't anyway. I haven't got my glasses with me. I can't see a thing."

"Do you mean to tell me you can't see a thing without your glasses?"

I thought Goldblatt would be angry, but he sat back in his blue leather chair with that expansive spreading movement I came to know so well and he said, "Oh really? Now that's very interesting, very interesting indeed. It's a mere formality. You don't really need to read it."

"But I do. I never sign things without reading them." When I looked through those inner windows again the girls were staring. I think that was the day I wore a chartreuse muslin tunic and trousers, with a silk veil over my face. That might have also been a day when I had drawn a caste mark between my eyebrows. I thought they were looking at my clothes but much later I wondered if they were listening to Goldblatt on some kind of intercom system and that they, like he, were anxious to get my signature on that document.

"You can trust me," said Goldblatt. "You don't really need to give it a moment's thought. As your mother and father would tell you, God rest their souls, I've looked after the family business day in and day out for many, many a year, Margaret." A long silence passed and all movement ceased in the outer office.   "And," he said, "it hasn't been easy, Margaret, not that I wish to complain. I do think though, in the realm of human relations, you could sign." And once more he waved the piece of paper under my nose.

"I can't," I said. "I can't see what it is."

Never, in all these skirmishes, did Goldblatt ever say anything about trouble with The Arsehole, though the day he told me about Gloria Thorpy he became almost lyrical.

"A tart," he said. "Highclass, mind you. Only by appointment. She's got a very lavish apartment just off King's Cross," he said. "Freehold. Every brick, every scrap of mortar owned by our Gloria. She was trained, Margaret, and I do mean trained, by a marvellous old woman who cut her teeth, so to speak, in the cat-houses of old Shanghai."

"I'm not sure I remember her very well," I said. "Gloria Thorpy, I mean. Not the old lady."

"Of course you do: very long legs, immensely long thighs, very tanned, very haughty expression, turned up nose, pale green eyes, extremely slim ankles — my goodness, is that the time? I mustn't keep you. Are you sure you won't sign this? I refuse to be offended, Margaret. I fully realise that the very many years you've spent living—" He stopped there. The way I have lived is beyond Goldblatt's comprehension. "Well, anyway, people won't hold it against you. Look at me, Margaret. Am I hurt that you don't trust me? Have I ceased to smile? Will my attention to your legal needs and wants be any less because of your lack of trust? No, Margaret. No. I forgive you." I found out later that he did some lay preaching for a charismatic sect.

The most lyrical conversation Goldblatt ever had with me was about Gloria Thorpy but he never mentioned The Arsehole which made me think at the time that my presence at the house provoked The Arsehole's intrusion. Later I formulated a more sinister view of it all.

I thought The Arsehole must have remained quietly in his little concrete bungalow on the western boundary of our garden, viewing the world through his yellow glass windows as if through bile. While my mother enacted her lengthy packing fantasies in the dusty corridors of the big house, The Arsehole must have simmered with resentment in his small house below the crown of the hill, perhaps looking upward to the blinking of one tiny light through the lawsonianas of the old windbreak. That is what I thought. My mother packed up everything in the house very slowly and relentlessly and must have worked mostly in daylight because the power bills for the period are negligible. I found them in an old filing cabinet, placed in order of date. The bulb in her bedside lamp was only twenty-five watts and those in other light fittings throughout the house were mostly broken so she must have saved power deliberately. Although out of her tree, she had the pine cones in order, so to speak.

"When you go up to the house," said Goldblatt when I first arrived back, "don't let anything surprise you. I believe the state of the place is —" There was the first of Goldblatt's many pauses. "Well, I'll let you judge for yourself. Coming

16

from where you've come from, you may view it with different eyes. I have it on very good authority that it's a mess, to say the very least. Your mother was not — how can I put it — your mother was not a well woman the last few years of her life. It took her the packing way, Margaret, the packing way. Now, my own dear mother, God rest her, went the ordering way. I had to pay a tiny visit to all the shops in town and ask them not to take any more orders from her towards the end. Once she ordered two hundred flax plants, individually wrapped, and had them delivered in the middle of one of Muriel's coffee mornings." Muriel must be Goldblatt's wife, I think. "Muriel," he says, "was far from pleased."

My mother's house was very large and The Arsehole's house was extremely small. Most of it was on one level, tucked into the hillside and it may have been damp in winter. Water would have drained that way. The Arsehole or some other earlier owner of the place must have had a tiny extension built at the back, a small summer sitting-room that could not quite pass for a conservatory and which was not linked directly with the house. To reach it The Arsehole and his family had to go outside, along a mossy path that must have been too narrow in summer and too muddy in winter. Having to traverse a path like that would not improve anyone's temper and The Arsehole would have trundled along there many times to reach the other part of his house whilst above, glimmering through the trees, would be the sight of my mother's place and all of it under one roof. No need to go outside to reach an extra room. Occupied by only one person, an elderly lady rumoured to be dingbats. Windows slowly covered by packing cases and crates. Lawns growing rank and free to lap the building with tides of small pale flowers and a flutter of seeds to renew the process the following season. It would be enough to make someone's envy turn to a disorder of the senses and then, finally, the sight of me on the Juliet balcony that opened out from Mother's bedroom might have made him take up his chainsaw in a kind of territorial lust. Why should they have it, he might have thought, and now I have to see an Indian whore on that upstairs patio flapping about in some silly robe. Thoughts like that might have come into

17

The Arsehole's head. Certainly he never would have invested me with the grace of a sari, the gentle benediction of my Indian tunics and my gauzy jacket sewn with gold. He would have thought of me as a tart wrapped in a curtain.

He was a man who was interested in gardening because he had a fine camellia hedge and polyanthus were growing well beneath his own trees, which he never trimmed — an ultimate injustice for me to view. One night, just before dark, I went down to the boundary to see what The Arsehole's garden was like. I wondered if his cruelty to me over land was mirrored in a devastation on his own section: motorcars harboured for parts and rusting on a rank front lawn, assorted bits of metal and wood for mythical building or repair jobs thrown in heaps amongst clouds of seeding sow thistle. Not so. It was a pleasant garden, like any other.

It was after the elephant came to the house, after I was given Wallace to mind, that I was brave enough to go down through to the boundary to view The Arsehole's demesne. Wallace stood behind me and I kept my right palm an inch from his knee, my voice just waiting to cry, "Hup, hup," so he would march forward. But it was all quiet down there. The remnants of an old post-and-wire fence straggled along beyond the lawsonianas to divide my mother's property from The Arsehole's and kikuyu grass had crept up this, straddling the posts and binding the wire into a kind of hedge. There was very little other growth under the trees because no light reached there and above our heads the branches swayed and sighed, a noise as faint as fright or the stirring of a little child at dawn. When I looked behind me I saw, covered with dandelions and rampant red geraniums, the buttock of the hill upon which my mother's house was securely planted, the curved front of the seaward portico as proud and bold as a set of teeth. I looked back at The Arsehole's house to see a hairy arm grasp the window catch of the only open casement and the window closed as silently as a lid may come down over a dead eye. The Arsehole had seen us and withdrawn. He would have shouted at me, as he usually did, if Wallace had not been there with me.

"Bloody rich woman in your great big bloody house."

That is what he used to say, and you cannot tell me that this is not jealousy speaking. We were interrupted in our viewing that night by Goldblatt on the telephone. The ringing penetrated the undergrowth, scattered the starlings that roosted above the door of the old shed. Wallace and I returned to the house to answer it.

"Just a tiny thought, Margaret." Goldblatt's voice sounds well oiled, as if he might have eaten oysters fried in their own golden batter for his dinner. "If I were to pop up to the house right now, Margaret, could you put a signature on that form for me, please?" He does not wait for a reply. "No need to read it, my dear. I'm sure those glasses of yours are hidden away somewhere in that great show of your mother's and not much chance of finding them I'd say. And no need, really, to bother. All I need is a little scribble along the bottom of one sheet of paper and then I won't worry you again. If you could just do it for me I could settle your mother's estate so very much more quickly. You could be out of that ghastly old place in about five minutes flat." Goldblatt stops to give a titter. "I exaggerate. But I could have you out of there in less than a week if you'd just sign this thing, my dear. I could have you out and away, miles from that neighbour you're always complaining about, by Friday. Even initials would do at a pinch. Have you heard the rumours, by the way, that it's haunted? Just local superstition and gossip, nothing to worry about, but you must feel a bit nervous up there by yourself. Can't say I'd relish the idea myself. Would it be convenient if I popped up for a moment? Say, in five minutes?" Goldblatt babbles on.

"You can do that." My voice is measured and Wallace's trunk lies along my shoulders like a loving arm. He puts his trunk through the pantry window and I grasp it as some might take a hand when drowning. "But I still need to read whatever it is, so you'll have to allow a few minutes for that." Goldblatt's silence lengthens. "I never sign anything without reading it first."

"Damn," says Goldblatt. "If I send Muriel over . . ." He seems to be thinking about this. "Muriel said to me just the other day, 'Barry,' she said, 'I must ask poor old Margaret over for coffee one day, or tea, or a glass of water or whatever

19

Hindus have in the morning.' I know she's been meaning to get in touch with you. Perhaps if I sent Muriel over, you two girls could have a nice little chat and you could pop the old signature down the bottom of this — well, it's really a most unimportant little document, hardly even worth thinking about by any intelligent person. Muriel could read it to you. What a good idea. Muriel? Muriel?" His voice is rising on an ascending scale of hope and aspiration.

"It's really no use." The pressure of Wallace's trunk is as heavy as that from an arm, as sweet as Christmas in a loving home. "I never sign anything till I've read it."

"Oh, well." Goldblatt sounds resigned. "Another time. We'll talk about it another time."

"But what about my morning coffee?" It is lonely in the big house all by myself and my mother's memories packed into moth-eaten cases are no company at all. Goldblatt has rung off, though, with the faintest tinkle like that from a thin old coin as it falls through a crack in broken paving stones. Goldblatt has gone. It is odd that Goldblatt always provokes the thought of money and the elephant prompts memories of love. An elephant was sometimes brought from the city palace to work in my garden in the north if there was something heavy to be done, if we had rocks to move or earth to be dragged in carts from one part of the grounds to another. On feast days I would have an elephant brought over so children who came to play in my garden could be given rides and Netta, prising my fingers from their little arms and disentangling those same sweet arms from round my willing neck, would whisper, "No, madam, no. The children must go home. You can't keep them here. Please, let go, madam, let go."

"Of course, of course." And I, remembering then, would go quickly indoors. Sometimes I believed, just for a moment, that one would stay. Perhaps just one tiny child, a musical child with long slim fingers, perhaps that child might stay.

Gopal, the man who looked after the garden, used to send for an elephant when we had planned major earthworks and Ranji would have one brought over through all the traffic in the city streets. The palace elephants used to move like royalty past all the three-wheeled carts pulled by camels, the buses full of tourists and other elephants bearing huge bundles of firewood or sacks of grain.

Up in the north of India the streets are full of animals that move with a nobility and charm that make motorcars look like grubby cats. I wish now I had taken more notice of how Gopal managed the elephant in my garden in India because now I would be better at managing Wallace here in my mother's garden that hardly ever, in her lifetime, saw the small beasts of the fields or the denizens of the day. Perhaps Wallace is the huge embodiment of all the small animals my mother sent packing from her flower beds in the days when the grounds were well manicured. Perhaps Wallace is gentle vengeance personified. If the holy man were here we could discuss this, and I feel sure he would attach some credibility to my thoughts. He gave me a little slip of parchment once and upon it he had written *However far my eye may wander you stand before me.* I wonder now if this means that Wallace is the essence of everything I once loved and that the idea and remembrance of love has come to help me.

After the evening telephone call from Goldblatt I fetch the canvas camp stool from Mother's wardrobe and I sit in front of Wallace contemplating his strength and bulk as darkness falls. The eyes of elephants are dark with mystery, damp with tears and I wonder if Wallace weeps for me and my need for tranquillity and wisdom. I am wiser in one respect, though, this particular evening. I know now that Goldblatt's forgotten Christian name is Barry. And that he is very anxious for me to sign something without reading it and the girls in his office and his wife seem to be part of the mystery as well.

Yesterday I managed to clear one of the downstairs windows and through it this evening came the light of the moon. Summer is ending. The autumn leaves have begun to fall, each of them like a small brown message from afar. *Your mother never loved you. You have no friends now. Everything you love and revere is far away and you will never see it again.* The dicta fall, bold as orders from a general, and I crush them as I walk. I might be saying, "I do not believe this." The soles of my feet, the arc of my toes might silently speak of my rejection of this negative series of thoughts as I go up to the house to answer the telephone again. It is ringing in the moonlit pantry, beside the kitchen. The pantry used to be a sort of cheerful entrance hall for that room and it was lined with jars of preserved peaches, all immaculately placed like yellow sickle moons in miniature, minuscule constellations of my mother's invented sky. There used to be ranks of pickles in brown jars, relish in containers of clear glass and beans salted in earthenware crocks. Only the crocks remain and these, in her ancient madness, she has packed with pillbox hats and matching kid gloves and sometimes artificial flowers made from hand-painted velvet, the stamens of finest silk. I had thought it would take a long time to unpack the larder but it was only a day's work. The moths and mice had settled there, made its dimness their base so I took most of the things outside and made a bonfire of them under a dead apple tree and the smoke rose through its bare branches like wisps of memory within the framework of remembered diffidence. We were not a loving family.

The telephone downstairs has a very long cord, as long as the tails of a hundred mice, and I have brought it into the pantry where I sit on another stool talking to Goldblatt again. It is an intimate small room, never altered since the house was built, so its wooden walls with their old varnish give conversations an intimacy as if I am speaking in the telephone box of an old-fashioned hotel. The real reason why I cleared out the pantry was to get at the window. It has a little window, a tiny casement as big as two dinner plates or a large box of chocolates, and it is this opening that I have wanted. I wanted to feel fresh air on my face. I wanted to see the moon. I required a ray of sun downstairs. The paucity of the window seemed to be all I could attempt, the boldness and sheer size of the big bay in the sitting room far too much for me to try at the moment. Beside this tiny open window I have pinned a note that my mother packed away with tenderness amongst her smaller hats.

Dear Mrs Harris, I'm sorry, my dear, I wasn't able to keep the navy-blue pillbox hat for you. It has been put on definite layby by Mrs Greig in Corsetry for her son's wedding on the ninth, but I have put aside a similar number in yellow astrakhan with feather trim and also a grape sou'wester shape, very new in the magazines, that would go with the suit you showed me. If I am not here when you come in, tell the girl they are in the big drawer second from the left by the windows. If there is a standing start for the Hillingdon Cup on Saturday please put ten bob each way on Achilles Heel, otherwise just place one bet on Ginger Magic, but only if there's been rain overnight. Otherwise Shirley Dear, the favourite, for a win. Yours sincerely, Mrs Rogers, Millinery.

I find this endearing, the fact that my mother had a friend in the hat department of a shop and together they plotted bets on race horses, within the clear framework of their friendship always referring to each other formally as Mrs Harris and Mrs Rogers. The sickle moon, shining through the pantry window, seems to smile on this idea. Wallace stands outside the pantry as I talk to Goldblatt and through the window comes his trunk to twine around my shoulders again so the day ends in a small triumph of love. My mother's note hangs from a drawing pin in the light of a smiling moon and it gives a warmth to the evening even though it was not intended originally for me. Perhaps, if we were to meet now, my mother and I could put bets on racehorses and keep it a secret from my father. I never call her by any diminutive, any fond name. I never did and my motives for doing this would be the same as those of anyone who stands behind the wire on a tennis court to watch the game, remains behind the curtains to watch a fight in the street. The upward strokes of all the letters that make up the words are like posts on a fence to keep sarcasm, injury and omission out, to keep reticence in. We were never friends, my mother and I, but her note glimmers on the pantry wall as much a message to me as the falling leaves in the garden and it says, "I was once a person." The mythical voice is very faint.

Goldblatt, tonight, is on full throttle though.

"Do hope I'm not disturbing you, Margaret, but the thought has popped into my mind that you might come across the odd valuable amongst your mother's things." I stand in the old pantry as quiet as one of my own dead mice and I hear Wallace munching an apple through the wall. He likes to stand outside the kitchen because I sometimes pass him biscuits and I also think he likes to see me working.

"Valuable?" I say, innocent as sixpence, telephone in hand.

"Yes." Goldblatt is relentless. "Valuable, Margaret. Or valuables, to be entirely accurate." There is a long pause. "I'm talking here specifically of, say, sovereigns. It would be like your mother, in her later years, to have ferreted away the odd sovereign in the odd little nook. And let me alert you to the fact, extraordinary though it may seem, that half sovereigns are more valuable than full sovereigns due to rarity. Less — or I should say — fewer were minted." Goldblatt is a man who likes to get everything absolutely right, particularly about money.

"Also there's the question of any valuable jewellery. Muriel has just told me that her mother says that years ago she remembers the odd fine little ring on the odd fine little finger, and not small stones either to coin a phrase, so if you find anything like that — gold, diamonds, small valuable items — bring them down immediately to the office. Safe-keeping, Margaret. Safe-keeping. We must always think of safety, mustn't we. You're very vulnerable up there in that great big show, not that I wish to alarm you. If anything were to happen up there nobody would hear a thing, my dear; you're miles from the road. You could call for a week and no one would come. As I've told you before, you could be out of the place in a few days if I just had this signature I need. Please, always remember I have your best interests at heart."

"Do you?" My irony is unintentional. Wallace is now relieving himself extensively on what was once the old vegetable garden and the sound is almost Italian, redolent of fountains in the heart of Rome.

"Indeed, yes!" Shameless in his enthusiasm for Mother's mythical gold, he presses to the attack. "Nowhere would your valuables be more secure than here, tucked away by my own devoted and entirely honest hands in my own personal safe." There is some murmuring in the background now. "Muriel says that her mother says the diamonds were the size of peas, my dear, the size of peas. They all remember them flashing over the bridge table like nobody's business. Cut quite a dash in her time, did your mother. Muriel sends her love, by the way. She'll ring soon. Bye bye."

24

CHAPTER THREE

SIX CITY COUNCIL workmen brought the elephant up to the house the week before last and that was three weeks after the day on which I appeared for the first time on the balcony upstairs. Within moments of seeing me in my yellow sari, the ochre-coloured caste mark between my eyebrows, The Arsehole came belting into the place with his chainsaw and hacked down the first of the camellias. More were to follow. Second on his list was a fine specimen of 'The Czar', not yet in bloom, but with buds that would one day have been flowers of deepest rose and ruffled like the collars of pierrots. The trouble had gone on from there so that, within a week or two, when I telephoned the police station to complain again of encroachment and depredation, the sergeant on duty just said, "Not again, Miss Harris, not again surely."

They brought the elephant to the house a good hour after a road gang began to tear up the pavement outside my gate. I say my gate but I had no sense of ownership there then, no idea of kinship with the building or the possessions therein. The gate always moved slowly on the old hinges. It might have been reluctant to let me in, and my filmy clothes used to catch on jutting nails, little shavings of timber not quite planed smooth, on the lock of the gate which often caught my fingers and pinched their tips till they were blue with small bruises.

By the time the elephant arrived the road gang had broached the bitumen with pneumatic drills and had erected an orange canvas hut over a hole they had begun to dig. From the doorway of this ephemeral little residence great shovels of earth flew forth from invisible hands. Dust upon the desert wind could not have flown further or bloomed so desperately against a sky filled with scudding cloud. It showed signs of being a stormy day. There was a lot of traffic. I had seen the lines of cars earlier when I began to unpack more of Mother's boxes covering a second window on the landing where I slept. I had been successful the day before with a cupboard under the stairs; it contained virtually nothing except for suit-cases that proved to be empty and one wooden box filled with old cast-iron casseroles with a speckled blue-and-white glaze, all of them in stalwart and sturdy shapes so they seemed to squat on the floor like friendly gnomes. If you live in a house too long alone you begin to invest inanimate objects with a humanness that could be a sign of loneliness. Where there is no company some is manufactured. It could be as simple as that. The row of casseroles with curved and grin-ning lids and nobs like noses had emboldened me so I thought, mistakenly, that I could open any boxes and would unpack them in a moment. And all the while my bonfires of what the mice and the moths had damaged beyond saving cast a pall over the neighbourhood, the smell of the smoke containing a curious fustiness as if I burnt the kingdom of the rodents.

As I opened up the third cabin trunk I heard a peculiar noise, a sort of airy blasting from some distance away, neither musical nor unmusical but on a high note of alarm. Wallace — if only I had known it at the time — was trumpeting at the traffic lights a block away. In the newspaper that evening the story on the front page said — well, never mind what it said. Negativism is often prevalent in small cities. I think they took a very negative view. Nobody was seriously hurt. The old lady who said she was on her way to the hospital anyway, as a day patient, to have a cyst removed from her right cheek had the right attitude, I thought. She did have six stitches in her face but, as she said, she would have had to have some stitches anyway. The incision was just made a little earlier, without a local anaesthetic, by broken glass from her wind-screen.

The photograph taken about a quarter of an hour later, through a telephoto lens, shows me greeting the elephant beside my front door, two policemen watching from a patrol car, city council officials mostly wearing suits and guarded expressions and the elephant stolidly planted beside a hybrid tearose rearing up above the weeds. In the picture I look like a thin foreign woman, my expression anxious and the long white scarf I had twirled round my head, the fair hair tumbling out the top like flames, has the odd look of an official turban, a foreign turban and not just a turban-like wrapping. I look like an albino Arab taking a holiday and the whole tableau has a dated air as if it happened years ago. Only the elephant has come out well, looking exactly like a charcoal drawing of an elephant by Rembrandt van Rijn in the British Museum. I saw it once when Stella and I went there to an exhibition of Indian jewels. Ranji had lent them some pieces of official regalia and Stella and I went to have a look. Stella said, "My God, that's exactly like Pinky." She had this elephant called Pinky that used to work in her garden and she would feed chapatis to him over the balustrading. Whatever they said about her later, she was a very kind girl to animals.

I remember we went off to Brown's Hotel after that to get some notepaper. We always had this joke, Stella and I, that we never bought notepaper. We only ever got it from Brown's Hotel, from the writing room off the main vestibule on the ground floor opposite the big sitting-room where you have afternoon tea. The commissionaire used to say to us, "And what can we do for you two ladies today?" because he knew us quite well. Stella often stayed there. "We might have some afternoon tea," we would say, almost in unison like two girls from a chorus line in vaudeville and, when you think about it, that is not unlike what we were. But all we wanted was the notepaper. It was just a joke, really. Meaningless. Like those women you read about in the paper now, the ones who knick a tin of salmon when they have more than enough money to pay for it. We just did it for the hell of the thing. You would say we were either bored or too fortunate, or possibly both.

Later in the evening we went to a concert in the Albert Hall. There was a pianist playing two Beethoven concertos and the notes dripped from his fingers, so clear and sharp I almost cried, and after that the orchestra played something by Benjamin Britten. Parts of it sounded like the noise electricity might make, and in the second movement the music rolled over us as if we were in the midst of fields of grain under a summer sun. Then it changed to the purring of cats, a grainy sound from the violins echoed by a bank of cellos and it ended in bewilderment with a melancholy and lost chord from the woodwinds. We never thought about it at the time, but I think that music showed us the map of our lives. We were then contented, settled, like the music that reminded us of happy cats. But it was to end quite soon. Stella's maharaja died and she had to go back home to London, to live in obscurity because there was a dispute over the will. The last I heard of her she was trying to sell her piano, and I imagine that if she cried as she did so it might have sounded like those horns at the end of the Britten work, the cadences so plaintive and faint that the music might have come from the desert far away or beyond the melancholy moon.

The trumpeting of the elephant when he reached the traffic lights was more robust, more a stating of claim, and by the time I looked out the upstairs window and saw him at the front gate he was walking with purpose, like a creature going home. Perhaps he scented the fruit on my trees, the flowers that still grew in drifts below the weeds, the water in the old birdbath, my friendlessness and despair. The sound of the road gang's machinery had already frightened me, but The Arsehole usually came in to do his felling in the evenings or at weekends, like a hobbyist who specialises in frightening women alone in large and derelict houses in his spare time. Whenever I heard the sound of saws or hammers I became suddenly very frightened. A great uncertainty had come to me by then so that day I kept going to the landing window cleared of packing and I would look out, like a creature beleaguered. But the men working out on the pavement stayed in the little canvas house flinging out shovels full of earth and it was only mid-morning, not The Arsehole's time of day at all. He had the back wall of his little house stacked up with firewood from the ground to the eaves and it was all from my trees, but he had accomplished this as an after-dinner exercise, as some people may take black coffee and a chocolate mint.

It was now just after ten in the morning and a crowd seemed to gather opposite my gate, swaying like a small field of corn on the other side of the road, a safe distance away. The odd airy noise, the trumpeting, came again, a little closer this time and from the crowd I thought I heard a baby wail, a thin sound and eerie as the violins in the Britten work so long ago when they struck a minor key to sound like electricity, or toothache. I might have imagined it, though. It could have been another of those seabirds that had fooled me so many times before.

A long line of cars had also formed on the road outside that day. I thought there must be a race meeting — the race course was only a block away — or an agricultural show, something to attract the populace for a picnic day. A voluntary and self-imposed obscurity had come to me by then. I did not realise that the crowd had come to see me. Or to be more accurate, to see me greet the elephant. There were still some smaller cartons on the floor under the second window I was trying to clear so I fell on my knees before them, as if devoted to the task, and began to tear at the lids. Sometimes my mother sealed them with sticky tape that had become flaky with age and other times she pasted whole newspapers or large sheets of brown paper over the tops of the boxes like seals on a tomb.

Unpacking things, by then, had become almost a nervous mannerism for me, a sort of tic douloureux. It was mostly books that day, wrapped up in 1940s underwear with the price tickets still attached, the cardboard yellowed with age. There were a dozen pairs of blue satin pants with flared legs trimmed with ecru lace, exactly the colour of snow on a doorstep at Gstaad when three people have walked over it in boots. The pair of knickers on the very top of the box was wrapped round a volume of reminiscences by the Duchess of Windsor, with her portrait on the cover, and that knowing face with its arched eyebrows looked out at me with all the sharpness of a wilful *fille de joie* of uncertain age and very certain tendencies. I thought I heard the trumpeting again then, very close this time. I put it down to too much imagination, too great a love of poetry, too much bending over trunks with the blood running to my head.

Wallace had become alarmed by the traffic. Although he was a circus elephant, his performances were always separate from his ordinary life. *Are* separate from his ordinary life. Past and present, present and past, they mingle into a pattern of performance and anonymity. Wallace would have merely thought he was out walking that day. He would not have expected a crowd. I tried to explain the psychology of it to the traffic officer who came up to the house a couple of days later to get my eye-witness account of the pile-up outside the gate. I told him I had seen very little, certainly not any accidents because I was reading the Duchess of Windsor's memoirs and he said, "Madam, do you know the difference between eccentricity and madness? Madness has no money and eccentricity has." He didn't even wait for me to answer. If I had I would have told him, at that time, I was chiefly rich in loneliness and rodent shit, not much else, but often you don't think of a smart answer till later, do you?

In the city where I was brought up, where I lived with this elephant I'm talking about here, they still follow fire engines. People will turn to stare at ambulances. Death attracts conjecture rather like that in the minds of customers outside old-fashioned butcher shops. Is the meat tender? How much is it worth? Will it cut up well? How long will it last? Birth induces the same febrile interest, but for differing reasons. Who did it? Is it all right? Is it all there? Has it got all its fingers and toes? Who is the father? They already know who the mother is. The day I sank slowly down on the pavement outside Kirkcaldie and Stains they did not know who I was at first, but the ambulance men looked in my handbag and found my bank book with my name on it. The mother is seldom a mystery. I was never a mystery in that matter, but I remember how my mother and father sat behind the screen round my bed in Ward Nine and I heard my father say, his whisper sibilant in the silence, "Has she said who the father is?" and my mother just said, with satisfaction, "Was, dear.

Was. They said it didn't even have fingernails. Too early, dear, too early, and all gone now. I think I'll go along to that room where they have a cup of tea for visitors. Are you coming, Athol?" Off they went.

The contingencies weighed up are always to do with suitability, economy and incertitude. My father often told me how much it all cost. Taxi fares to and from the station. They went by train to see me. A warm coat for your mother due to Wellington being much colder, at that time of year, than our own dear old Hillingdon. Two lunches at the hotel. Three nights' accommodation, and we were never sure the sheets were changed daily. The odd little thing that caught your mother's eye in the shops. And so on. Quite a crowd gathered, you know Margaret, and your mother was very upset when she heard about it. I thought it best to divert her. She just bought one or two items but they served to take her mind off things.

The crowd on the day of the elephant's arrival had followed the cavalcade from the botanical gardens where Wallace had been housed in an aviary for free-flying birds, mostly natives. I found this out later, by reading the paper, but nobody told me anything at the time. It was a mystery to me and I proceeded that day with innocence. I continued with my unpacking. Perhaps the people scented scandal, insurrection. Perhaps they seized at the topic of the day. The bird enclosure had several large trees and a small stream meandered through. In all, it covered the area of an average-sized section on any city block, and there Wallace had remained, placidly chewing leaves and yesterday's buns from the bakery up the road while droves of fantails fluttered round his big ears and tuis sang over his head.

A circus had had to leave him behind just before Christmas because one of the carrying trucks broke down and they had no other vehicle of sufficient axle weight to transport an elephant. There was also talk of trouble with money, near bankruptcy. It was one of those small circuses that does the rounds of larger towns and smaller cities in December to cash in on holidaying children, grandmothers wanting to take little darlings out for a Christmas treat, that

31

sort of thing. Ranji used to say I was the most innocent person he had ever met. I thought, the day the elephant arrived at my place, that the road gang had suddenly shut the canvas door of their little canvas house because the wind had sprung up. I thought the crowd had gathered because there was a race meeting on. Ditto the line of traffic outside.

I was busy sorting out the cartons, Mother's detritus of the years firmly wrapped in yellowing tissue paper and here and there I would find a piece of aged soap, often also yellow and in the shape of a lemon, an expensive variety which could only be bought in chemist shops from artificial fruit cases whose smooth white planks were filled with scented wood shavings. Stonelike and faded, with a faint bloom of mould on the skin, they gave the air of a mean carnival to the bathroom where I kept them in an old basket behind the door. They lathered quite well but their look of atrophy, the cracks upon their outer skin, gave bathing a deathly jocularity as if I were baptising myself in a necropolis. The bathroom had a domed ceiling, once painted pale green, and bleached now to faintest eau-de-Nil. Long mirrors on the doors of three wardrobes in the room — Mother kept clothes everywhere — reflected the aqueous light, the looming bulk of the big white bath that stood on ball-and-claw feet and the sight of me, a naked sprite made vert by the reflections in the looking glasses. I might have been something made from bleached malachite; and always holding a cake of Mother's lemon soap to hint at a peculiar harvest, a fruity cornucopia of neglect and decay.

Outside the window the leaves of a magnolia rustle and its leathery foliage and creamy flowers remind me of the butter trees in Bengal, the recollection of them and their lardy seeds like a journey in the mind from continent to continent regardless of logic. The bathroom at my mother's house seems very Indian in its gloom. Once I swam in a maharaja's pool filled with water the colour of verdigris and above my head were ancient garlanded swings where, long ago, earlier concubines hung like parakeets. In my mother's bathroom the same atmosphere exists, in miniature, but the festoons are cobwebs or old memories like that of my father's voice saying, "We have had to bring our elder daughter home; a

32

woman of twenty-six. Ridiculous at her age. She should have had more sense. You would think, wouldn't you, that someone of that age might know how to look after herself, how to get herself out of trouble." And now I am forty-six and still ridiculous, but my father's voice has gone and there is only me here, and the cobwebs and the yellow lemon soap, and an elephant arriving at the front door.

I had complained to the sergeant on duty at the police station several times during the past fortnight.

"Can't you do something," I had said. "Surely a person can't come into another person's property and cut up their trees for firewood?" So they had come up in a patrol car and they brought a policewoman with them who took me aside.

"We could arrange counselling," she said, a pale fair girl who looked as if she understood nothing.

And when I said, "But why should he have counselling?" she gave me such a bland and cheesy look.

"No," she said, "for you, counselling for you."

I went back into the house after that. I watched them and they waded down through the weeds to the old windbreak, where the lawsonianas groaned over their heads in the breeze from the sea. They stood looking at the pile of firewood stacked in The Arsehole's place and one of the policemen idly kicked the bright stump of one of the felled trees. I saw them laughing, though perhaps they were laughing about something else. Perhaps they had been laughing at some joke or another before they arrived at the house and were just continuing with mirth already begun elsewhere. The wise man from Agra told me once that the angry man can be overcome with gentleness, the miser with generosity, the liar with truth, so I waved to them from the balcony in gentleness, truth and generosity, and I watched them laugh again.

"A boundary dispute," said one of the constables when they came back to the house, rang the front doorbell so it sounded like a titter echoing through Mother's packing cases. "We don't usually find there's a lot we can do, not with boundary disputes."

"But it isn't a boundary dispute." I could already see them looking over my shoulder into the gloom beyond, into the hinterland of rodent city where every time I mopped the floors, dried and flattened tiny carcases of mice were collected with the balls of dust. "There is no dispute about the boundary. The trees are mine. He just keeps cutting them down, that's all, and I want him to stop."

"But your neighbour—" and here one of the constables consulted notes on a clipboard, "I can't quite read the name, he says he owns the land the trees are on. Your neighbour says he's merely felling his own trees. He says that shortly, in a week or two when relatives arrive to help him, he's going to clear all that." He waved an arm towards the biggest grove of rhododendrons my father ever planted. "He says they've got problems with shade in the winter, and moss and so on, and it's all going to be cleared as soon as his father arrives."

"And his brothers," said the policewoman. "He's got three brothers." She smiled at me so brightly and brilliantly, like a person with inner knowledge. "My sister's engaged to one of them."

When they drove away, the patrol car skimming through the weeds of the drive like a shark on the bottom of a sullied sea, she leaned out the window and said, "Do think about the counselling, and I'm not sure if we told you, but your neighbour says would you take all that stuff out of his shed because he wants to use it himself."

"Shed?" I felt suddenly faint, as if the sari fluttering in the breeze was my own flayed skin, my flattened heart held up for laughter.

"Down there," she said. "The shed, the shed with the green roof down near where he's cut his firewood from; he wants those old lawnmowers cleared out of it and all that old spray and stuff. It's a filthy mess but he's been kind enough to give you a fortnight to get it cleaned up." I must have looked shattered, like a helpless lunatic clad in a few strands of unsuitable silk and standing amongst the weeds. "He's got the family arriving in a fortnight so you've got till then." They drove away.

"Goldie", my voice on the telephone is desperate and fear makes me almost intimate, "Goldie, something terrible has happened."

"Just one moment, Margaret." Goldblatt's voice is confidential. "I'm just seeing off someone now, another client. I'll be with you in a tick." His voice becomes louder, rises above the secret whisper. "Well, goodbye, Charles. Very good luck with the business. I feel sure everything will go very, very well for you, even though eighty-seven per cent of all small enterprises fail within the first year." He takes a huge gulp of air. "Kindest regards to the family. Do tell Raewyn, Muriel's going to ring her and get her to pop in for coffee sometime. Best regards to your mother. Oh, sorry. Just slipped the old mind for a moment, remarkable woman. We always said she'd live for ever, but of course none of us do."

The whisper returns and there is the sound of shuffling. Goldblatt is getting himself settled at his desk again. "Margaret, whatever's the matter? It isn't like you to telephone the office without an appointment. And what is his name?" he wants to know when I have finished my recital of depredation, encroachment and theft. "I don't really think it helps, Margaret, if you become abusive."

I have now told him that I do not know the neighbour's name. I merely refer to him as The Arsehole.

"The Arsehole isn't much good, Margaret, in trying to identify the culprit. An appellation like The Arsehole doesn't appear on city council ordinances, Margaret. I'll be unable to find such a name in the Land and Deeds office, now won't I?" There is another of Goldblatt's long silences. "By the way, has Muriel rung you yet about that coffee morning? I'm just thinking, it might be nice if you and Raewyn met. Perhaps she could have you together."

"But what about The Arsehole?" I want to know.

"We'll knock him into shape," says Goldblatt. "Never fear. Now I'll just get one or two particulars from you and you can leave it with me." There are some scratchy little sounds now, perhaps a pencil on rough paper. "Just a few tiny calculations, Margaret. I'm estimating now that if he claims your windbreak so he can cut it down for firewood and if he also claims your mother's garden shed and that area of land between the shed and the actual boundary, I'm calculating now that he's got his beady little eyes on about half an

35

acre of your land. Fascinating, isn't it, human greed? Anyway, leave it with me. And before you ring off" — so I'm going to ring off, am I? — "have you found any sovvies?"

I am absolutely lost.

"Sovvies? What are sovvies?"

"Sovereigns, Margaret. I was talking to you about them the other day. I feel sure your mother must have salted away gold up there. Anyway" — he sounds quite blithe — "keep an eye open, Margaret, for coins and in the meantime leave this little probbie with me." Goldblatt is very cute today. "Remember, my dear, there are no such things as difficulties in life. There are only little probbies to be overcome. I'll ring the city pound and the mayor's office and see if I can get you some sort of guard dog up there. I think if you had a dog there you might find this Ar—" He stops himself there. "You might find this neighbour may pull in his horns. I'll give my brother a ring. He works up at the zoo. They may even have a dog up there they can spare. Vandalism, you know Margaret, is a great problem for them. They have four or five Dobermans, as far as I know, it could be more. Perhaps Bernie can spare you a Doberman, or they might have one at the city pound, unclaimed. We'll see what we can do. In the meantime, my dear, never fear. Ever onward and upward." I wonder where Goldblatt learnt to talk like that.

"Thank you, Goldie." But I am very humble because I am frightened. The idea of The Arsehole claiming the garden shed, the lawsonianas, the rhododendrons and half an acre of my land in the middle of Hillingdon, has crushed me. "Very good of you, Goldie." We are suddenly into fond diminutives, now, Goldblatt and I. "I can't tell you how grateful I am. I'll look forward to the dog arriving. Perhaps Mother's got a big box tucked away somewhere that I could turn into a kennel with a little blanket and things." I, also, am becoming cute today.

"Bye bye, Margie, and try not to worry. I'll ring round about a guard dog."

"Bye bye, Goldie, and I'll watch out for sovvies."

So that is how I got the elephant, and a city council official is holding out a piece of very thin rope to me now — the cavalcade has reached the front door — and he says, "For you." The elephant's eyes look as if they are filled with the sadness of many lifetimes and the skin round them is damp with tears, his toenails as big as empty dinnerplates held in the fragile hands of the starving.

"Deliveries of food every day at nine a.m. Any problems, ring the director of the zoo. He's away on holiday till the twenty-fourth but he might be able to help you after that. We simply can't accommodate him any more and you've lived in India so you'll know all about elephants. Good luck."

"Thank you." My own thin and anxious hand stretches itself out to take the cord. I seem to have little control over things today, except aged lemon soap and dried mouse carcasses. The hand moves of its own volition. When they have all left, after the photographs, I realise I do not even know the elephant's name but I think, perhaps, I might be able to wear the blue satin pants, with ecru leg lace, as riding clothes. I see myself, atop the elephant, patrolling my boundaries. Add too much imagination to my crimes. The elephant just stands there, gentle, huge and apologetic. He wears a crown of bird shit on his head and his back is saddled with dribbles of dicky-bird lime, the lines of it as mysterious as Sanskit and almost luminous. It is the loneliness that makes me like this, seeing unwritten messages everywhere. I know that. If Netta were here with me, Netta whom Ranji sent to be my companion, I would have someone to talk to. I would not think trunks and boxes said, "Your mother never loved you. You are not wanted here, and never were. Everything you loved has gone." I would think none of that. Florid and byzantine thoughts of the divided heart, pungent reminders of my secular upbringing with all its ambiguities, my chronicle of a life's minuet in a maze of mirrors, would not exist.

As darkness falls on the elephant's first day at my house I am hosing the bird muck off his back, clambering up his side on the old step-ladder from the kitchen with Mother's red rubber hose, almost perished but still usable, in hand and I am scrubbing the elephant down with a broom from beneath the stairs. The street outside is empty. The road gang has folded up the hut and gone, the hole filled in. The crowd has dispersed. I never heard the ambulance. I did not see the fire engines. The wide flaring legs of the satin knickers cling to my thighs as I scrub the elephant down.

"Wallace," I say to him. "You can be called Wallace." He has a look of charm as if he understands the skills of the card table, the mysteries of the boudoir, the life of a libertine. So I name him after Wallis, Duchess of Windsor, author and subject of one of the books upstairs and, because I am absurdly correct in small things, I give him the masculine form. Wallace. Greater and more important correctnesses escape me. As the moon rises on his first night at my mother's house, I sit in front of him on Mother's camp stool and I begin to read to him just as a mother might read to a fretting child. We have already been on the first of many daily patrols round the boundaries, The Arsehole's house in brooding silence with a light shining at only one window and a silver Mercedes, sharp as an exclamation mark, parked in the drive. While I watch I see the front door open and for a moment there is the vignette of Goldblatt, oily smile like a smear, handing an envelope to The Arsehole.

It is many years since I turned the pages of the little book I wrote for the holy man, and the ivory covers creak as I open them on the story of how I went to India. The journey from the zoo, through all the traffic, has made Wallace nervous. He has begun to trumpet again, that airy sound of terror and bewilderment, but as I begin to read he becomes quiet, docile. It soothes him. I might be his mother and he my peculiar child. My voice rises and falls, my sibilance whispers in the gathering dusk, and the *histoire* of the journey begins to unravel amidst the drifts of sow thistle, wild periwinkle and strappings of honeysuckle that bind the herbage of Mother's garden to the dark earth. As my voice ascends, thin as the song of a lark, I see again the black eyes of the holy man, irises flecked with gold, as he hands me the pen and paper.

"Oh, sing to me, dreamer," he said, and I began to write.

THE FIRST READING

I stole my father's car and ran away from home one night in early autumn when the moon was full. I drove out the gates and left them open behind me, swinging in the wind. I had one small bag with me and that contained only a book, a novel. I was a librarian then and it seemed logical to take a book with me although I left everything else behind. There is a theatricality in everyone's temperament and I may have been influenced by another book, a novel I once read about a woman who ran away from home without even a tooth-brush, and lived to regret it. So I took a book with me, just for the sake of taking something. I never regretted anything, which shows that real life does not always emulate literature, though the critics say it does, and literature has a life of its own, which is how myths are made.

My own work still lay on my desk down at the city library. Someone else probably finished it. They may have kept it aside on a shelf, like an appendix in formalin. The book she was working on before she ran away. The exact pen she was holding as she worked on her last day. What she said on her last day. They might have looked up at the shelf, at the book, fearful as turkeys at Christmas, and they might have said, "That is the exact book that drove her mad." It may never have gone into general circulation. It was not intended for it, anyway.

I had been covering and cataloguing an art book with portraits of Indian maharajas and, prophetically, their women. It was to go into the permanent collection at the library, in the section where weighty volumes were kept in glass cabinets and you had to ask for the keys to the doors if you wanted to research anything. It was to be in that department and by morning tea time on that last day we had already had an argument about whether it should be under the amorphous title A for Art or should fly in beneath the gaudy banner, M for Maharajas. They may never have put it into the library system at all because twenty-four hours later I ran away with a maharaja I had only just met. They might have left the book to be covered with dust as a liver may be drowned in a solution of formaldehyde. This is the book that caused the trouble. That is what they might have thought.

My father, portentous in the corduroys he usually wore to golf, might have declaimed, "I blame it all on that book."

And there would have been a lot of conjecture round the town. What had happened to my father's new Cortina, his pride and joy in eau-de-Nil that matched his upstairs bathroom. Why was it returned a week later by an Indian fruiterer from a very distant seaport? Where is Margaret? When is she going to reply to our kind invitation, under the circumstances, for her to join the tennis club to meet new people and be taken out of herself? Never. I could have told them that when their note arrived, but my mother placed it on the hall table like an accusation and it had already begun to curl and go yellow when I left.

A picture of a beautiful Indian woman was in that book, a portrait painted in Lucknow in 1786. If I close my eyes I can remember her face. She sits on silken cushions, leaning against a carmine bolster with tinsel tassels. Behind her is a marble wall. In the distance, over the railings of a balcony, stretches a limpid landscape with trees, roses and arches of pink stone. The expression of this beauty is serene. She is perfectly composed and regards the jewels on her fingers and arms with equanimity. Those hanging from her ears would have been just a sensation of weight, swinging from the pierced lobes, the feel of jade and pearls warmed by her own flesh. I did not know, when I first opened that book, that one day I would be just like her except my hair is fine and fair and grows in ringlets so I used to tie it on top of my head with jewelled circlets. When I worked at the library I tied up my hair with ribbon, black ribbon, and when I told Ranji this he had circlets made for me of onyx and rock crystal.

You may wonder why I worked at the city library in the town where I was born when it is plain I liked neither the library nor the town. At the age of twenty-seven — I was twenty-seven when I ran away to meet Ranji — I should have established myself as an individual elsewhere, in a milieu of my own choice. I should have had my own place, my own things to do. I did have them once. I had all those things, and when I lived in my father's house that last summer I grieved for the loss of them. A woman of twenty-seven does not sit easily in her father's house, or not a father like mine. She does not take kindly to being told what to do and, in my case, I was told every day in subtle ways of my errors. So they were always new and fresh. Nothing was forgotten in that house except peace and joy, which were states of mind he regarded as an extravagance.

40

He was a conveyancing lawyer. I think now he was a bad lawyer, mediocre in his thinking; he must have been to have employed Goldblatt to represent family matters.

"I see another nuisance is out of the way," he used to say when he read the local newspaper. There might have been a report of a prison riot, a convicted murderer stabbed in the mêlée with a sharpened Biro. "Less for the taxpayer to foot the bill for."

Once I said, "Fewer. Fewer not less," and out of the corner of my eye, at the very edge of my peripheral vision, I saw my mother leave the room, but he just said, "What?" And he went on turning the pages of the paper.

"Heigh ho, let's see what's happening at the Basin Reserve," he said. Or it could have been Athletic Park, The Oval or anywhere. He was mad on sport, following cricket and Rugby with the simian avidity often possessed by the incomplete or the faintly incapacitated. During the war he had had his right leg amputated below the knee, not as the result of a war wound, but after he fell off his bicycle and gangrene set in. I never knew my grandfather, but he evidently was similarly maniacal about all sport and had been born with only three fingers on his left hand. According to family legend, they were alleged to be very alike in every possible way though my grandfather's wife died very young, which, I think, could have meant that she was cleverer and more sensible than any of us.

I have often wondered about the couplings of my mother and father. They produced two daughters. I used to think there would have been few preliminaries, and those would have been rudimentary in the extreme — just some obligatory removal of smaller garments which my father would have folded carefully, or even hung up. I am not sure about my mother. Possibly she would not have folded or hung up her own clothes, but my father, in that case, would have spent twice as long attending to the clothes because he would, then, have looked after hers as well. Later procedures would have been silent, speedy and almost surgical. My father would then have read the sporting news in the paper, some of it aloud. My mother may have slept. Again, I am not sure about her. Perhaps she wept. This is all conjecture on my part, but I knew them so very well I feel it may be true. It would not be completely false, at its worst.

Like most lawyers, my father had mastered the arts of impression and inference and wove them into his daily life. I used to hear him talking to my mother while I cooked dinner. It was my job to cook dinner, allocated to me from the very first day I went back there to live with them, and while I cooked I used to hear their voices ebbing and flowing, rising and falling. They were like grimy tailors endlessly mending soiled garments, the words of these discourses like scabs over sores that remained untended.

"I see she got home all right on the bus." There would be a rattle from the newspaper. My father would be flicking over news, editorials, personals — advertisements from the lonely or the bereft left him untouched — seeking the magic of sport.

"She caught the second bus, not the first. The half-past five, not the five-fifteen." My mother, the telltale, was always specific.

"The second bus? Why the second bus? Why not the first?"

"Ask her yourself, Athol." Snip, snip. That would be Mother cutting the wool for her latest tapestry. She embroidered cushions with winsome kittens disporting themselves on antique stools, gardens redolent of roses and hollyhocks with church spires in the distance, always imaginary landscapes, or interiors, of sibilant innocence. Snip, snip. The scissors again.

"Why did you catch the second bus, Margaret, and not the first?" My father is at the kitchen door now, his eyes assessing. I might have accomplished elaborate mating rituals with total strangers behind the bus stop in the few minutes between departures.

"The first bus was full so we waited for the second one." I am peeling potatoes and the skin of them falls like pieces of pale flesh upon the white tiled top of the bench. Everything is tiled white in my father's kitchen as if it is a mortuary and in a sense it is. It is the scene of our constant dismemberments, not the tearing of our actual flesh, but the cutting of our thoughts, the setting adrift of separate perceptions.

"We?" says my father. "And who, may I ask, is we?"

"I." I continue to peel potatoes, the skin dropping now like a series of cold thoughts. "I meant I caught the bus."

"But you said we, Margaret. Both your mother and I distinctly heard you use the word 'we', Margaret. The plural. We."

"I meant I caught the bus. Some of the other girls from the library were at the bus stop, but they caught buses to other streets. But we were all at the bus stop together which is why I used the plural 'we'." The fun is going out of the game now. I have lost heart with the business of teasing my father to death with how long it might take a quick fornicator to indulge at a bus stop whilst awaiting the five-thirty. For this is what my father thinks, you see.

I remember when they both sat beside my bed in Wellington Hospital and all my father said was, "I really do not see, I really and truly do not see, how she found the time. I've looked at her timetable and I cannot see how there was time." And he looked round then as though searching for arithmetic in the air, calculus in the smell of ether. "I do not see how there was time for all this. If you had managed your time correctly, Margaret, this disaster would never have happened."

I just said, "Yes." You get very weak, in every possible way. It seemed hopeless to explain to him that time had nothing to do with it. It was not a matter of being quick or slow. It was a matter of wanting an A for my essay on finite element analysis of incomprehensible material within the literary framework of the Brontës. I felt, at the time, that my father would not understand this and in retrospect I think I made the right decision.

"When you come home, Margaret, we must ensure that your time is fully organised. We cannot have this again. We cannot have a repetition of this. We cannot, your mother and I, be expected to travel up and down to Wellington at the drop of a hat."

My father was in his courtroom modus that day. It was an applied psychology he never used in real life except upon his own family. At his office he merely did conveyancing in smaller property deals and attended to the legalities for various large companies.

"I'm sorry, Margaret. I do apologise." There is no apology in his tone now, though. "Your mother and I are merely trying to—" He goes no further. It would be difficult to state what they are trying to do. Perhaps they are trying to get an evening meal at a reasonable time. Perhaps they are just trying to get a free cook, for life. "I was confused by your use of the word 'we'."

"And frightened." This is my mother calling out now. "Confused and frightened."

"Now you've frightened your mother." My father hastens back to the dining-room. My crimes are multiplying, innocently, with every passing moment. I return to the job of cooking the dinner after this investigation of the lying witness, the exposure of cupidity,

43

vulgarity and sexual congress of the most inconvenient sort result-
ing in travel arrangements being made at times not chosen by the
travellers, inferior shopping and the odd little parcel to be
unwrapped later.

I went away from that house when I was very young and studied art and literature at university. Then I stayed on to do my doctorate, or that is what I told them. Eaters of a bland diet (tonight,
for instance, I am labouring over potato salad with bought mayon-
naise, sliced ham with tomatoes cut simply in quarters), possessors
of lives in which remarks are not made so this passes for peace, my
parents would not have understood my real reason for staying on,
for continuing my studies. The truth of it was that I could not stand
the idea of living with them again and I really had never thought of
what job I wanted to do. So I never told them. My father thought he
divined it, of course. I heard him say once, "Margaret seemed to have
formed a most unfortunate liaison with some kind of academic. He
was, of course, married. They always are." But I only wanted an A.

It seemed a simple ambition at the time but when I walked along
Lambton Quay on that last day, though I did not know it was the
last time I would walk there then, I was aware only that I felt off-
colour, that it was not one of my better days. That I felt ill. That I
sank slowly down on the pavement outside the main doors of
Kirkcaldie and Stains. That I lay on that pavement and could not
get up. That someone came out of the shop, a girl in a pink overall
with the name of a cosmetic company embroidered above the left
nipple, and she said, "The ambulance is coming. Please don't cry,"
and I had not realised till then that I was.

"We will never be able to shop there again," said my mother, an
interesting and revealing remark and she, also, wept as she uttered
it. Perhaps she wept for the loss of the bright lights (Hats, for
instance, had crystal chandeliers in Bohemian glass, not English),
the jerseys in ranks in the knitwear department, matching kid
gloves within glass-fronted oak drawers in Accessories and all the
secret glories of Underwear.

It is an odd thing, but the lonely will misconstrue the vaguest
interest, the meanest invitation to the smallest gathering, the most
grudging compliment, as love. To the professor — and I always
thought of him as that; I do not know whether this is to my credit
or denigration — I would have been only one of a number of girls

he had. Dozens. He might have had dozens or hundreds. I realised that later. My mother thought I had become broken and docile when I just said, "Yes," as soft as a gasp when I heard her say, "Couldn't you have popped round the corner, Margaret? I mean," and here she cleared her throat as if I were to blame for bronchitis, influenza, all infections of the bronchial tubes, "there was the side door, Margaret, by Hardware. Couldn't you have managed to get to the side door?" I don't think my mother ever ventured into the hardware department. Hammers and nails, brooms for the yard, nuts and bolts were not her sort of thing. "It was a most unfortunate choice," she said. I think she meant the location of my collapse. I said, "Yes." I agreed with her.

It was most unfortunate, the whole thing, and the most unfortunate thing about it was that I had mistaken lechery, ambition and intrigue for love. Perhaps I had spent so long studying books and their characters that I thought in real life you could somehow write a happy lovely autobiography for yourself by your own actions, and also inscribe a happy ending. I see that as my great error. I was too literary. I had thought life could be written. I never finished my essay, of semi-thesis length, so the Brontës and their incomprehensible material remained incomplete. I discovered, very swiftly, that I had plenty of incomprehensible material of my own. One thing I could never comprehend was that, disregarding the venery of the situation, the professor never loved me and I thought he would simply because I was me.

One of the other girls was not as lucky as I had been. Perhaps degrees of ill-luck were all we achieved. She died. An overdose of sleeping pills, half a bottle of whisky and Beethoven's Fifth Symphony playing over and over again on her stereo. As far as I know the professor continued to live happily with his wife and three children in what the real estate agents would call a commodious California-style bungalow with all the grace and charm of yesteryear coupled with discreet refurbishments to bring it up to a totally modern standard. They were busy at the time of my collapse with plans for an in-ground swimming pool, heated by natural gas, when in-ground pools heated by gas were new. I do not think that the words stupidity, cupidity, venery and silliness would have been used in any of their glossy brochures but they were certainly engraved on the mythical monograph in my own head.

45

When I went back home to work in the library I found there was something very melancholy about pushing the big trolley loaded with processed Returns round the shelves. It was like a tour through the painful doleurs of my own personal bill of indictment, and the way the titles fell was often another castigation. As I Lay Dying, Fate Is The Hunter, Assignment to Catastrophe, A State Of Seige, Owls Do Cry, For Esme With Love And Squalor, The Heart Of The Matter, The Remains Of The Day, After Julius. It seemed like a varying statement of crime, and all committed by me.

I recall the last time I ever spoke to the professor. I telephoned him from the hospital. You had to go downstairs, to another ward, to use a pay phone. It seemed a long way.

"Please, Margaret, please," he said, "don't be a nuisance," and as he hung up I heard, very clearly, the laughter of children in the background, and the sound of hammering. Perhaps the changing pavilion, in the French style with hand-carved finials and a mansard roof, had already been started by a team of better builders working under the aegis of the most superior firm of landscape architects in the city.

The professor always claimed that his wife was much older than he was, he had married her only for her money and that she did not understand him.

When I subsequently worked at the library I discovered that this is a very usual old series of mendacities and I also discovered that lack of knowledge of it was yet another of my many crimes. As well as thinking I could write a pretty life for myself I had also read too well. My reading was too good, of too high a standard. I had never perused turgid rubbish, the lower end of the reading scale. If I had ever had a holiday job on Returns, with specific interest in Light Romances, I would have been a wiser person much earlier. Even Westerns or Rental Adventures might have illuminated my mind about the lack of honour amongst rustlers, the saucy deceptions of bordellos built in the mud. The path to the professor's study went through a shrubbery and was muddy in winter. My essay, as I planned it, was to be a long one. Need I say more. If I had been a dim-witted reader with a flashy taste in lack of literature I would have been a cleverer and more street-wise woman. My exalted choice of books — nothing of a lesser stature than Joyce, and

Brookner only for the holidays — ensured I was naïve to the point of cretinism. When the professor said, "My wife doesn't understand me," I said, "That must be very sad for you." I should have said, "Don't give me that load of balls." Stella Mudge's father was on the high wire, at the sawdust end of show business, and Stella has taught me a flinty line in dialogue. Sadly, I have learnt it too late. For the professor, anyway.

The women I worked with at the library were much older than I was. I had no friends there. You lose touch with people. Hillingdon was a place people left, each present generation only appearing in photographs on mantelpieces or with their names inscribed on certificates of prowess framed and hung over upright pianos in the sitting-rooms of proud mothers. This is our oldest son Bernard who works for a big company in the Persian Gulf. No, we haven't been to see him yet. It's so difficult leaving Grandma and we aren't good in the heat. This is our daughter Julia who's in the corps de ballet. She was always such a dainty little girl. We always said she'd have a very bright future. And this is the poor Harrises' daughter Margaret — she had a miscarriage on the pavement outside Kirkcaldie and Stains one March day, right outside the main doors. Such a promising scholar. They had such hopes for her. It was so very public. You couldn't miss her. The poor Harrises were never the same again. That is conjecture on my part. I feel sure I was never mentioned like that but they would all have thought such things. In their clumsy tactfulness they expunged me from their conversations and committed the atrocious unkindness of not acknowledging my existence. So I was lonely there. I was lonely at the library and sometimes I used to think about the friends I had at university. There was this girl who had the cubicle next to mine in one of the halls of residence and she had a fetish about washing. She'd squat on the floor with her clothes in a bucket of soapy water and she'd scrub them for hours, till her knuckles ran red with blood. I think I know why she did that now, though I was less wise then due to my exalted reading. If I had read worse books, less literary treatises of the human condition, I would have been much more practical much sooner. The other girls said she'd spent a bit of time with the professor the previous term.

There was also a man, a friend of my father's, who used to ask me out to dinner when he was in Wellington on business. He was

*old enough to be my grandfather. My other friend Louise — she was
a cousin of the one who did the washing — said one day, "What do
you do," and I said, "What do you mean — what do I do?"*

*"For God's sake, Marg, are you half asleep or something. What
do you think he asks you out to dinner for then?"*

I said, "So I'll eat it."

*"Don't be bloody mad." She came off a farm and her language
could strip paper off the walls. "He's only asking you to dinner
because he wants to go to bed with you. What else do you think he's
buying all that fillet steak for."*

"Last time I had chicken," I said.

"Stop splitting hairs," she said.

*I sometimes think of all that. I was about fourteen weeks preg-
nant at that time. He was quite an elderly man. He might have been
delighted. "He's quite an elderly man," I had said to her and she
said, "My God, aren't you ever going to wake up, dreamer?" People
often called me a dreamer.*

*"It's the last thing in a man to die, don't you even know that,
you poor silly cow." He might not have been so picky about the
dates. He might have sent me a bunch of flowers. He might have
said a bit more than, "Please, Margaret, please," if I had telephoned
him from the hospital. It would all have ended up the same anyway,
on the pavement, so none of it matters.*

*When we went to our lectures the professor, from the podium,
would declaim, "The sonnets of that great master, William
Shakespeare, have as their essence self-love, Narcissism if you like,"
and he would glance at his own reflection in the glass doors before
darting a look at me. I thought it was filled with love but probably
it was contempt. I have never been very talented at telling the difference. Perhaps he was gazing at the girl behind me. She was the
one who killed herself with the whisky and the pills.*

*There is no need for whisky and pills here. People die in the
streets. So I have been told, but I have not seen it myself. Pills are a
luxury here. There is a doctor who runs a clinic over by the market
and there pills are wealth. I have seen a mother carry a child away
from there, a screw of paper containing just one pill in her hand like
a talisman to show the way through the night. If that girl had lived
here she could have taken her bottles of pills and given them to that
doctor to save the innocent and would, thus, have been given her*

48

own life and innocence back. Beneath the wide, warm and luminous sky of northern India she would have found better things to do than die over a man who lectured on Narcissism and practised it himself beneath his manifold mansard gables. The same firm of architects designed his wing at the university and his pool pavilion and the buildings had a marked similarity, but the pool house was much smaller and the audience there was more scantily clad.

There is a great freedom in writing this account of my journey for the holy man who has come from Agra. I drift. I drift in subject just as I have always drifted in life and in my thoughts. I have now drifted far from my father's stolen car and my journey to meet Ranji. Perhaps the holy man is correct in his belief that I have not acknowledged my passage from the inner reaches of my father's house to the outer provinces of India. I discuss the departure and I talk about this rosy city but nowhere are there any thoughts about the journey. In this expulsion of the facts must lie the origins of my desolation. That is what he says, the holy man from Agra.

I drove out my father's gates wildly and much too fast. I nearly hit the gatepost when I set off. If I had been as wild and generous with myself as my mother claimed I was, I would have left before the sun was up while my parents still slept, on their backs, behind brown holland blinds with ecru fringes while their Westclox alarm, in sensible cream and green enamel, ticked away on the bedside cabinet. They had a dressier little clock in blue enamel, and I mean jeweller's enamel now, and sterling silver but they seldom used it though it could be set as an alarm. It was kept on the dressing table, as an ornament. I do not think it was often wound though they called it the good clock and the other one just the clock. They called my sister Sylvia the clever one and they called me our elder daughter Margaret. The blonde one. Perhaps some meaning can be drawn from this.

They had a four-piece bedroom suite, not the usual three. Do not forget that he was a lawyer in a small town, my father, and in such places there is much distinction between people who own three-piece bedroom suites and those who have the extras. Their suite was in burr walnut, solid not veneer, and the bedside cabinet was the size of a child's coffin with a carved apron and an elaborate brass handle to the door. If I had been truly as careless and bold as my parents made me out to be, as bold, say, as the carved acanthus leaves on the door of their cabinet, I would have stamped out their gate into the

49

bountiful landscape in the early morning. I would have been wearing my mother's best pearls and would have had a huge handful of notes taken from my father's safe, which I would have spent on taxis to a distant spot. I had felt very friendless there, and the most dangerous moments in life are when you need a friend. Perhaps if I had had friends I would not have left.

There was a bountiful beauty in those hills around the town. The town itself was not lovely, set on a series of dark wooded ridges that led to the sea. But when I left, daylight was fading and, even though a great golden moon was rising, I saw very little of the place. I have no last memories of great sights or wonderful views. With my own quaint brand of precision, I had left impetuosity till the very last. I waited till my mother and father left for the bridge club in a taxi they shared with some neighbours and I remember a raddled little blonde woman with carmine lips shrieking at me through the window of the car, "Don't do anything we wouldn't do," the words bubbling as if through blood.

"Velda's always so sharp," my mother used to say. Velda of the carmine lips was sharp. She was the sharpest person I ever saw and always wore sharply cut two-piece suits in acrylic fibres that took luminous dyes. Shocking pink, glinting lime green, luminous orange — all these were Velda's favourite shades and she glowed, the night of my departure, in a slightly foreign irridescent ultramarine. My father, glum in a brown tweed suit, sat in the back seat, in the farthest corner with the small man who was married to Velda. I think now that we never even dignified him with the appellation 'husband'. He was forever untitled. Even my father only ever referred to him as 'that little chap who's married to old Velda'. Her brightness and sharpness had whittled everyone away and their only daughter had fled to be a missionary in Outer Mongolia: a journey I emulated myself to a different part of the globe, following different deities. You would have to do something drastic if you lived with Velda and I suppose it was logical for me to do something drastic simply because I lived with my mother and father in Hillingdon. The holy man says out of darkness we are led into light. My father's house was certainly very dark and the light here is like that inside a pearl.

"What time will you be back?" I bent down to talk through the windows of the car. I could see they took this as a kindness, as good behaviour. My parents exchanged a glance. *She is knuckling down,* I could imagine them thinking. They often said I should knuckle down.

"Don't wait up, dear." My mother patted my hand, which I had placed on the car like a fleeting invitation for my own exit. "You're such a good girl." She was turning now to the others. "She's really try—"

"Drive on," said my father so the taxi slid away.

Trying to make up for it, my mother might have meant. Trying to make up for the business on the pavement, for Kirkcaldie and Stains and the ambulance at the main doors, the job in the local library as an assistant.

"But she can work up," I used to hear my mother saying on the telephone to her friends, perhaps to Velda of the luminous dresses. "Only an assistant at the moment but there's no end to what she could do, with her qualifications. She could, of course, go back and finish her doctorate, but Athol is dead against it."

Before I hurtled out the gate in their beloved eau-de-Nil Cortina I stopped for a moment, listening to the noises of the night just once more, and I heard hedgehogs snuffling in the grass near the gateposts. I was still immured in the better type of literature then and I imagined, wrongly, that even the hedgehogs wept for me. They were probably looking for snails, or piddling. If I had read *Rental Romances* more thoroughly, if I had studied them as well as I studied Thackeray, I would have had my mind solely taken up with whether or not I should have lipgloss with me, whether I should have had a little talk about various things with the doctor before I departed, whether the doctor was handsome or not and possessed melting brown eyes which made my heart beat faster. Many of the turgid tales seemed to be about doctors. If I had read them I would certainly have been wiser, if not actually cleverer. I blame myself for everything and place my magnificent taste in reading at the axis of the problem. My foot seemed to caress the accelerator then, with this series of cankerous and cancerous thoughts, and the tyres of the car spun in the gravel. I might have been a robber leaving the scene of a crime, and it was a crime to leave my father's house like that, to take his car. He had been so kind. Everybody said so.

"Your father's been so kind." I used to see deeply into the irises of people's eyes as they bent closer to me. "We do hope you realise that, Margaret. Your poor mother and father have been very, very worried." I would be getting the tea trolley ready with supper for one of their bridge parties. There was always someone who wandered out to the kitchen to have what they called a word with me. Usually it was several, and all of them in long sentences. "Your poor father's been a very worried man. Underneath that bluff exterior, Margaret, there lurks a heart of gold." So it was a crime to steal his car and drive away as the moon rose, to bolt off from a house where the silence was as telling as thunder.

My father came back to Wellington to collect me from the hospital and we left the ward in a thunderous silence. He carried my suitcase while I trailed along in a bathrobe. I think he took my things in his hands to make sure I did not drop them, and I noticed as we drove through the city on the way north he took a route far away from Kirkcaldie and Stains and its varnished main doors. Never forget for an instant that I sank down in front of the main doors. If it had been beside Hardware I do not think my father's silence would have been so brooding, my mother's injury so complete.

I have already told you that the moon had begun to rise, a huge generous golden orb. It was so bright I forgot to turn on the lights of the car. A solitary policeman shone his torch at me, swinging it to and fro in an arc like the flight of a small night bird. He was standing on a street corner in a country town much further down the highway and it was only then that I knew I had rushed forth in darkness. Secret and reticent as always, I had gone out on to the roads like a vagabond, unheralded and unlit. Only the moon had showed me my mad, bold, nervous way through the night. Round my shoulders I had tossed a chintz opera coat that was actually my mother's and its fine wide collar was folded round my throat like the crumpled wing of a butterfly. So I had dressed myself for my own private and absurd operetta of charm and delight.

No pleasure or gladness had come to me during the previous months when I tramped out that gate to catch the bus to the library, watched by my mother from an upstairs window. In the beginning, once or twice, I waved to her but there was no answering salutation. It was then I knew that my mother watched me to make sure I actually got on the bus quickly and with no escapades behind Mrs Somerville's prize hedge of clipped Australian bottlebrush bushes.

It could have been a pleasant journey, just a few blocks on the bus to the library where I worked in the book binding department as an assistant. Not so.

"But she can work up." My mother's voice echoes in my ears like the sound of blackmail. "If she wants to."

The night I took the car and went off on the first part of my journey to meet Ranji, I laughed. I was happy even though the thought of such a migration made me afraid. I chose between life in a dark, still house and a long journey on a stormy night to an unknown destination, and the destination won. The holy man says that a pure and strong will is all powerful, and in my infinite wilfulness I simply and most powerfully wished to be happy. The perception of what I had been allocated and what I wanted — what I want — became a source of meditation as I drove through the night, and the difference between the two has become my continuing fever.

It is the season for dust storms here now. The wind whirls across the desert and we keep the shutters closed. The sky and the land are the same colour, the horizon blurred by sand suspended in the air. In my house the marble walls have a bloom of fine grit, the inlaid patterns almost obscured. Tawny agate and dust match almost exactly so the fine etched traceries of vines and flowers on the walls of my rooms disappear in the heat of each day and return only in the evenings when Netta creeps about with a duster made of embroidered muslin. She strokes the walls as if she is dancing slowly to the music of the night.

It is not a time of year when it is easy to think. I have not got us very far along the road south, the road I took when I left my father's house, and it is not easy to recall it because I forgot it as I travelled even though I went, innocently, into the eye of a storm that has become a legend.

CHAPTER FOUR

"ARE YOU SURE you're warm enough?" Muriel Goldblatt's eyes are ringed with purple pencil, deeply fringed by eye lashes tarred with mascara and the skin beneath her high arched eyebrows is pearly with ivory blusher. It is exactly eleven-fifteen on an ordinary Wednesday morning and outside, on the main road, the traffic is hooting and roaring up the hill on the outskirts of town. The Goldblatts live on a ten-acre block and their house sits on a hilltop, a vast bay window in the early Elizabethan style, like an architectural paunch, sagging on to a newly formed rose garden. Muriel and I are sitting on a velvet love seat within the cavernous interior of this glassy gizzard and we are watching out for Raewyn.

"I feel sure you'll really like her," says Muriel. "Raewyn's a real live-wire. She's a lovely person, very out-going and very caring. Raewyn's a really wonderful person. Barry says that she's the real strength behind Charles. Without Raewyn Charles wouldn't be anything, Barry says."

"Does he? Wouldn't he?" I am not sure what to say about all this. It is not what I am accustomed to.

"You're very quiet, aren't you?" Muriel Goldblatt sounds a bit desperate. We have been sitting for half an hour in the bay window looking for the elusive Raewyn and there has been no sign of her. "Barry told me you were very quiet. He told me—" But the telephone is ringing now and Muriel hastens through the inner reaches of this vast room. "Do excuse me."

She clatters away over the slate floor which, here and there, has silk hand-woven rugs thrown over it in places where no one would walk very often. Thus is richness and parsimony balanced in the Goldblatt household. I sit on the velvet love seat and its grip is far from fond. The cushions are made of pale blue pure silk, matching the upholstery exactly, and they are outlined with scratchy lace. Nothing seems to be very comfortable at the Goldblatts' place. From far away, from the entrance hall, where I saw a telephone on an imitation Chippendale table treacled with bold reddish French polish, comes Muriel Goldblatt's rising voice.

"But she's already been here for half an hour," I hear her say. "Well, why can't Raewyn come?" So Raewyn has let her down, I think. Raewyn, the live-wire, won't be turning up today. "Yes, Barry," says Muriel. "Yes, darling. I will. Yes, darling, she is very quiet, just like you said." Muriel sees me leaning forward and we exchange glances through the open doorway. We nod and smile, as if we are enjoying ourselves. "Yoo hoo." Muriel is waving to me. I wave back.

"Yoo hoo, Muriel." My voice is soft and unconvincing, though. All these conversational signals are foreign to me now. The game is beyond my comprehension. If I were visiting Stella I could talk about the Nizam of Hyderabad's greasy old hat that he always wore or what exactly happened to Prince Sayajiao in the South of France in 1985. But here, I do not know what to talk about here. I have forgotten the game that is played here, if I ever knew it.

The drive up to the house clings to the side of the Goldblatts' hill and I stand now in the bay window looking down towards the road and I wonder how will I get back to my mother's place again, how will I go home? I am trapped at the Goldblatts' now. The taxi left me at the gate.

"Don't think I'm taking my car up there," the driver said when we arrived. "I brought someone here last week and never again. Never again. Don't ask me to go up there." The Goldblatt residence loomed above us and from below the big bay window looked like a giant eye, a watching orb that stared at my progress in amethyst-studded ballet shoes as I trudged up through the gravel. The sound of the taxi was already fading as it took the merciful road back to town and Muriel Goldblatt's voice, bold as a bandsaw, echoed in my ears as I took the last perpendicular bend. This is an exaggeration. It was not quite perpendicular. Add exaggeration to my list of crimes.

"Barry said you weren't a great one for sensible shoes." Muriel's melodious laugh makes the blackbirds rise from their perches. As I draw closer I see the chatelaine of Château Goldblatt is more than six feet tall. Her thighs, although in perfect proportion, are as big as Doric columns, and if her arms were roasted and served with apple sauce they would feed a regiment.

"How wonderful to see you after all these years, Margaret." Muriel takes a giant stride forward. "I remember you so very well. We were at school together. You were in the sixth form when I was in the fourth." She kisses my left cheek with a mouth as big as a cushion, glimmering with lipgloss and with the lips either outlined with orange pencil or tattooed. The effect is overwhelming. I am clasped in her arms, engulfed in the heavy scent of Chanel No 5 which can be intimidatingly worldly early in the morning. Muriel's well-modulated voice resonates in my ears.

"But you were always very shy, and I never knew you very well. You were in the Professional Course, in A Block, over by the tennis courts, and I took Commercial. The Commercial girls were in C Block, in the middle of the school buildings, near the gym. Do you remember the time when . . ." I have been led into the house like a tortoise, for I am moving slowly, on a string, Muriel's memories, in vivid detail, passing over me like incomprehensible commands on foreign stations where even the English alphabet does not have a place and where the trains are never on time.

"How frightful." This is all I can manage to think or say and the remark, ridiculous and archaic, has squeezed itself out of me involuntarily. I might have had nothing to do with the words at all. A dog, lying under one of the rose bushes, is the only thing that looks warm-hearted, but Muriel Goldblatt has followed my glance and rushes forward. I am left standing in the cobbled forecourt of the Goldblatts' extravaganza as Muriel chases the animal away.

"Frightful indeed," she shouts. "Just some sort of a ghastly bitser from the farm next door. It keeps coming into the garden. Barry gets absolutely furious about it." The dog has run behind one of the Goldblatts' gigantic fence posts and we exchange a glance, the dog and I.

"Has it gone? I can't quite see."

"I think it ran away down the hill." The dog and I exchange another couple of glances. I am as protective as an adoptive mother, a pathetic woman who makes surrogate children of any animal she happens to see. "I think I definitely saw it disappear into those trees." I wave one arm towards a stand of bush and Muriel prepares to usher me into the house where the unloving love seat awaits and also the faint and very faraway scent of coffee which smells too weak to be sustaining.

"I've invited Raewyn," says Muriel Goldblatt. "Barry says you wanted to meet Raewyn. Barry says he thinks you must have been at school with Raewyn. We were trying to get it all sorted out. Barry says he thinks that Raewyn — Raewyn Chandler that was, you'll remember the name — he says she was in the fifth form when I was in the fourth and you were in the sixth. I think you were a bit older than we were."

Muriel pats her hair which falls in a smooth bob, soft as down, each strand of equal length. It swings like a curtain as she moves. My own hair is very long by now. It is weeks since I left my house of pink stone and Netta, who cut my hair before feast days with a pair of big silver scissors the old princess once sent from Biarritz. My hair is fastened today in a vertical pony tail on top of my head and strands have begun to fall down.

"Won't you sit down?" This endless discourse has led us to the two-seater sofa into whose comfortable depths I cannot sink because there aren't any. I remain, lodged, like a frightened chicken on a perch. We are deeply enmeshed in the animal and bird kingdoms today. "Won't it be marvellous to catch up on old times," says Muriel. "And wasn't it terrible," her voice is lowered now, "about that accident when Esme Burrows had her leg and, I think, one ear cut off. Esme was in the third form when you were in the sixth and I was in the —" I have ceased to listen to the voice. I have no recollection of any of this and the name Esme Burrows means nothing to me.

"Perhaps you didn't hear about it in India, Margaret. India's quite a long way away." Her smile is confident and serene. "Anyway, it was a long time ago," Muriel says. "I wonder where Raewyn is. She's usually so punctual." The silence lengthens. Muriel coughs. "Barry said you were very quiet. He told me no one could get a word out of you. That's why we thought Raewyn might strike a chord. She remembers you so well. Her name just sprang into our minds immediately. And there's Gillian Mackersey too; I wonder if you remember Gillian Mackersey? She's had a very sad history." Muriel Goldblatt is beginning to babble. "She was the other woman in a very distressing triangle. The wife committed suicide; we think it was the old hose-in-the-exhaust-pipe-of-the-car routine but nobody was quite sure at the time. And then the man married Gillian but the last we heard he'd had a hip replacement and she had to have a hysterectomy — some kind of awful abdominal emergency in the middle of the night — and neither of them was in very good health. I wasn't quite sure how to get hold of Gillian. Someone said they'd gone to live in Thames but the curtains still look the same at their old house and we've never heard they sold it. No one knows what to think. It is all," booms Muriel, "very mysterious."

Over Muriel's large shoulder, past the belly of the gaping windows, I can see the signs of an old scar on a distant hillside. Once, a long time ago, the whole face of that escarpment must have slipped gently into a ravine, trees and all. A coppice has come to maturity with everything at wild angles.

"What's that down there?" The golden discs on my jacket tinkle as I raise my arm to point at the lunatic forest that grows, laced with wild clematis, almost parallel to the ground. It is a luxurious woody scene and the noise the golden circlets on my jacket make is also a reminder of luxuries that are uncomprehended by the Goldblatts.

"Oh, that." Muriel is dismissive of the curious forest below her windows. "That's just an old land slip. It happened years ago. Barry's had it all surveyed and it's perfectly safe. There's no danger of any subsidence. You must remember that terrible storm, that hurricane we had once? It was years ago, years and years ago. Were you here then?" Muriel, at last, is pouring the coffee which is, as the scent suggested, far too weak. But it is hot and I am becoming a desperado. I snatch the cup from Muriel. "I feel sure you aren't warm enough, Margaret. There doesn't seem to be much warmth in that little tinsel jacket you've got on. Shall I turn the heater on? Your hands are blue with the cold, Margaret, blue with the cold."

"It's quite all right," I say. "It just seems rather chilly here, after India."

"Of course." Muriel speaks quickly, as if I have mentioned a naughty habit.

"And as for that storm you mention," I am like a person hastening to the attack, or one eager for punishment, "I was here, and I wasn't. I drove through it the night I left. I just thought it was very windy. Sometimes the car almost seemed to lift itself off the road as I drove along ridges. I thought it was very strange that so many roads were being torn up by road gangs who left lanterns round holes in the highways. I couldn't understand why there were no people about, why there was hardly any traffic. I thought I was driving very badly and that's why the car behaved so strangely. It nearly went off the road on bends. I couldn't seem to steer it properly. I didn't realise till much later, when I read about it in an old newspaper, that I'd driven through a hurricane. I went through the eye of the storm. It was such a terrible storm, such a cyclone, that there was even a photograph of some of the damage in *The Times*, did you know that? News of the storm got as far as London."

Muriel has been silenced by this outburst. She remains standing beside another imitation Chippendale table, slightly smaller than the one in the hall, and her big white hand clasping the handle of the coffeepot looks as if it, too, is porcelain, possibly an ornamentation from a tomb figure for one of the larger pharoahs.

"Your mother and father," says Muriel, "would never talk about it." The tone is austere. If Muriel were to be turned into a dog she would suddenly be a big golden Labrador with a heavy sonorous booming bark. Woof, woof woof. That is Muriel, the dog, barking in alarm and admonishment. "It wasn't a thing anybody mentioned very much. Your mother and father were very respected people in the town. We all wanted to spare their feelings. Your father, as I understand it, was president of Rotary at the time and he stood down, Margaret. He stood down. He gave up his position because he didn't feel it was suitable for him to carry on. Everyone felt very sad about it."

"I didn't." The dog, my sudden child, has filtered back into the garden and is lying under a rose bush again. The holy man from Agra said to me once, "Who is dumb? The man who cannot say a kind word at the right time, Highness, that is who is dumb."

"Anyway, do have a biscuit, Margaret." Muriel is holding out a basket of shortbread. "Or would you rather have a sandwich?" Muriel looks at me, helpless as a gauche girl. "I'm not sure what Hindus have in the morning, actually. Would you rather have water?" I clutch my cup of warm weak coffee. "I didn't know what to do about the eats. Barry said samosas, but I didn't know where to get any. Not here, anyway."

"Coffee and biscuits are fine, thank you, Muriel, but if I have a biscuit, am I allowed to do whatever I like with it?" Already my cold blue hand is stretching out to the basket. The dog would like a biscuit, I think. The dog looks as if he needs a treat.

"Of course you can, Margaret." Muriel's laugh is uneasy and she has become watchful. "What an odd thing to say."

"Excuse me, Muriel." I am leaning in front of her now, opening a window to hand the dog my biscuit. "I know you won't approve of this, but at this exact moment I really feel I'd like to give my biscuit to this nice dog."

"Who is rich?" asked the holy man all those years ago. "The man whose heart is contented, Highness, the man who can see the soul of a dog."

"But I am not a Highness," I told him.

"But I have been told to call you Highness. Highness said,

when he brought me from Agra, that you were to be called Highness also."

"You always were a very funny girl." My title is altered now and Muriel's laughter is not humorous. It is almost bitter. "And you haven't changed. Barry told me —" But here we are interrupted by the telephone again and Muriel clacks away in her high-heeled shoes to answer it.

"Yes, darling," I hear her say. "Yes, Barry, she's still here." There is silence for a while. Barry must be talking at length. "Oh, fine," says Muriel in a bland and innocent voice. "We're getting along just fine, talking about old times. I told her about poor Esme but she can't quite place her. Anyway," the voice becomes conspiratorial now, "I'll tell you later. I'll tell you all about it later, Barry. Later, darling, later. And, yes, I'll ask her. I'll get her to do it before she goes. Yes, darling. I'll lend her mine. Yes, darling, I won't let her go without doing it."

I have left the Goldblatts' window open and I pat the head of the dog while Muriel talks on the telephone. My golden jacket tinkles again, faint as bells down in the market. Last year, when Ranji first became ill, he sent the goldsmith to my house. I had not known he was coming to see me. There was this little man ringing the bell at the gates that led to my own courtyard, and when I said, "Yes? Yes?" he held up the scales from his knapsack, scales to weigh gold so I knew then what was going to happen. Through my binoculars I saw that all the windows and doors on the very upper level of the City Palace were closed and I knew what the news would be, what the doctors who had been brought from Delhi had said. I knew it all when the little man in the dhoti held up the scales and I ran up all my stairs to the highest cupola with the binoculars in my hand.

I comprehended everything exactly when I saw that those very private upper apartments, the rooms where the princes had always conducted their private lives, were in darkness. In the darkness of my own house, behind shutters closed against dust, light and enquiry, the goldsmith worked with ingots brought by a beggarboy through whose rags I had seen a flash of scarlet silk, the bright livery of those distant

61

towers I watched through my field glasses. On the first night I saw the light from a small lantern on the highest balcony, as if someone had come out from one of the dark rooms and stood for a long time looking towards my turrets and domes. Then there was nothing more. I never saw anything more, but the goldsmith continued to produce bright discs like giant sequins patterned with strange runes and devices, and Netta sat with her needle and gold thread mixed with linen for endurance, and she sewed them on to a cloth-of-gold coat that was already heavy with woven bullion. It was a treasure house in secret guise, like a stock-in-trade someone might take on a dangerous journey, but I did not think of that till I began to travel.

Muriel comes clacking back over the squares of slate. Her shoes are high-heeled mules in dyed reptile, with bows at the front.

"It was just Barry, ringing me about a little job he wants you to do." She is pouring more coffee for me, handing me another biscuit. "I'm quite worried about you," she says, "being so cold. You really need a nice warm coat." Muriel seems to be considering me as if I am a candidate for redecoration. "A nice navy blazer," she says, "in fine wool. My mother's got one and she finds it endlessly practical, goes with absolutely everything." The saucer eyes narrow now. "And so smart with red, and a touch of white." Today I am wearing a pair of mauve silk trousers gathered at my ankles and over these I have a matching tunic that ties at the neck with ribbons encrusted with pearls. They are real, of course. Baroque, faintly pink and very large. Like my jacket, they are part of my simplistic banking system and seem far more valid, to me, than the figures on statements from obscure Swiss banks that I have tucked away under the lining of my portmanteau.

"Pastels aren't very in this year," says Muriel, "and all those lolly colours. According to *Vogue* it's all primaries this year. Your reds and your blues with a touch of white at the throat."

My hand stirs at my own throat. I have forgotten what I am wearing round my own neck, but there is definitely something there and I have had it on for several days. I have bathed myself in the green and dusty chamber at the top of

Mother's house and have gone into the water, jewels and all. Yes. My hand finds the pendant warmed by my own flesh and I know now that I am wearing jade set with square-cut emeralds. Muriel peers at me again.

"Green," she says. "Most unusual. I don't know whether I'd ever be brave enough to wear purple and green together. I must tell Barry." There is Muriel, the big Labrador again, going woof, woof. "I've never thought a lot of jewellery during the day is very necessary." Woof, woof. As I stir faintly under the weight of these veiled admonishments my matching bangles clink and they sound like tin teaspoons tapping the sides of cups that are not porcelain.

"They don't look real," I said to the goldsmith when he made them for me. "That is excellent," he said and never looked up from his little crucible for a moment. "That is safer for you, Madam," and with that one word, Madam, I learnt, yet again, that my journey from my pink house had already begun in the minds of the people.

"Just a little string of pearls or a wooden bangle does me. I feel that's quite sufficient for most people." Woof, woof. Here is Muriel, the Labrador, again. "Anyway, it's nothing to do with me. You're quite at liberty to wear whatever you like. I'm sure we'd all respect what you chose to put on, even if most of us wouldn't dream of wearing saris and all that spangled stuff in the daytime. But I do worry about warmth, Margaret. I worry that you don't seem to be very warm. Barry has voiced the same concern to me, Margaret, and to others. He's a very caring person. Raewyn is actually his third cousin. I forget the actual relationship, it's something to do with his maternal grandmother being married twice." A final woof. "Anyway, do think about the wisdom of buying a nice warm blazer and, meanwhile," she is tick-tacking away again, towards a desk on a distant wall, "I must get a pen. Barry says I've got to get you to sign something. It won't take a moment, and then I must ring you a taxi. You'll want to be going home, won't you."

"Yes." The way I shout the word it sounds more like YES-YES-YES. "Yes, I want to go home. Yes, please ring me a taxi. I'd like that very much indeed."

63

"Woof, woof." That is the actual dog underneath the pouch of the Goldblatts' artificial mullioned windows. As I give him more biscuits Muriel is rummaging around in a writing table made in the Louis Seize style. The varnish is like toffee to match the artificial beams in the ceiling and an enormous brick fireplace looms nearby with gothic niches for photographs from which the faces of several children beam. The Goldblatts' offspring, I think. The line is certainly not going to die out.

"If only I could find my nice Parker," Muriel is saying. "I can hardly get you to sign with a Biro, now can I?" Rummage, rummage. Muriel, the dog, has stopped woofing and is now digging for a bone. "You look so serious, Margaret," she says, tossing the words over her shoulder like rags, "I do wish I knew what you were thinking. Still waters run deep, that's what Barry says."

"I think that's what's known as a trite saying." My baby, the dog, is looking through the windows and his open mouth and pink tongue make him look as if he is smiling again.

"A trite saying?" Muriel is still searching through the contents of the desk's drawer. "I must tell Barry. He'll be most interested to know it's got a name. Ah." She stands up very straight now, pen in hand, and advances towards me. Muriel the Valkyrie, in full flight. "Found you, you little devil." With a large piece of paper in her hand, snatched from under a paperweight on the desk's overblown inlaid top, she advances towards me. "Barry says will you just pop a tiny signature on this and," she takes her own glasses off the top of her head where they have acted as a bandeau for her hair, "I'll pop these on for you so you can see. Now do just sign at the bottom of the page and Barry'll be so very thrilled." Her big hand obscures the words.

I am effectively blinded. Muriel's spectacles, awry on the end of my nose, present me with a view of the world that could be that of a dying beast, perhaps a cow already at the abattoir. The treacle varnish of the Goldblatts' furniture fades into a dark haze of dried blood from dying kine above a forgotten horizon. The floor, as I turn my head, undulates. I might have been suddenly set down on an ochre sea. Muriel looms above me like a big tree, like one of the lawsonianas in Mother's garden. She bends over me. Now she looks as if she is a tree being felled by The Arsehole.

"Have I told you about that man, that peculiar neighbour of mine, who keeps coming into the garden and felling trees?" I ask. "That's why Goldblatt, I mean Barry, got me the elephant."

"Barry told me you jumped from subject to subject in conversation in the most peculiar way." The dark shape of Muriel is retreating. "So I was prepared. I'll just ring you a taxi, Margaret." The sea undulates a bit more and the tree reappears. "Just let me guide your hand, Margaret, if my glasses aren't much help. What a pity. Perhaps we haven't got the same kind of eyes. I'm very short-sighted with a hereditary astigmatism. What's the problem with you?"

"I'm long-sighted." I am beginning to feel nauseated and I lie back on the hard silk cushions. I am seasick in the Goldblatts' floating landscape and, as I move my head again, the room heaves to the left. I close my eyes. Muriel places the pen between my fingers and puts my hand on the page.

"It doesn't matter if you can't really see it properly," she says. "Barry says it's of no importance, a mere formality. Now, pop a little signature there, dear," and this 'dear', this endearment, frightens me, "and I'll ring the taxi for you. You'll want to be going home."

"YES, YES, YES." I have said it again and as Muriel clatters off to telephone for a taxi I fold the sheet of paper in three and I am holding it like a fan when she returns.

"Oh, goody." Muriel is talking like a girl in the fourth form. "How super. Barry will be pleased." Snatch. The page has gone from my hand. Bang. It is slammed into a drawer of the desk, which Muriel now locks and puts the key down the front of her dress. "Must keep things safe, mustn't we?" Woof, woof. A roguish Muriel leads me out into the garden. "I must show you my handmade concrete teddybears, Margaret. I do think they give a very creative atmosphere to the garden, don't you? Barry says I'm a very creative person. If you look carefully at each bear, Margaret, you'll see they're all slightly different. No bear is the same as another,

Margaret, isn't that wonderful? I do think creativity's very important in life, don't you, Margaret? Next year I'm going to classes in making photo frames out of granny prints. You could come with me if you like. Raewyn and I go together. Last year we went to tap-dancing classes, after we'd seen *42nd Street*. I don't suppose you saw *42nd Street* did you, being so far away?" Muriel prattles on. Something is making Muriel nervous. We have got as far as the front veranda now.

"What do you think of my terracotta pots, Margaret? I like to have something in them as a feature and then smaller things, like lobelia and alyssum cascading down the sides so it looks very naturalistic. Sometimes," and she bends over and pulls at a disobedient frond of daisy growing upwards instead of down, "I'm not sure whether I've got it quite right." Occasionally she darts a glance back at the house, at the pot-bellied sitting-room with its locked desk and the artificial mullioned windows with panes of distorted glass tinted yellow to hint, at nightfall, of a jolly golden welcome at an Elizabethan coaching inn like something on a Christmas card.

"Yes," I say. "No. Yes-no. No-yes. Um." Muriel does not notice this lack of communication.

"And these are my 'Super Star' roses, not at their best at the moment, I'm afraid. We've got this very bad outbreak of blackspot and yellowspot and we don't know why. Barry," says Muriel, "is calling in an expert, a marvellous man by the name of Bartholemew. I'm not sure whether it's Something Bartholemew or Bartholomew Something, but I suppose you wouldn't have heard of him in India anyway so it doesn't matter." A large arm gestures to a swathe of bushes. "And over the other side, over here, Margaret — no, this way, dear, this way. You're looking the wrong way." My gaze creeps to the house, to the mullioned windows beyond which the desk sits boldly on that cold slate floor. And in the desk is the sheet of paper I have not signed and I am wondering — when will the Goldblatts find this out?

"These are my 'Sexy Rexies', such a wonderful col—" Muriel interrupts herself. "Oh, Margaret," the relief is intense, "I think I can hear your taxi now. They don't wait long. I think you'd better run." So I am, thus, relieved of being on Goldblatt duty and I take off down the gravel drive like a keeper of the watch on holiday. The dog has been waiting where the drift of 'Super Stars' fades away into indeterminate plantings of hebes and he runs beside me, mouth open as if he is grinning.

"Taxi for Goldblatt," the driver calls as I slam the gate behind me.

"No," I am jumping into the back seat now, "taxi for Harris, ordered by Mrs Goldblatt," and we begin the journey back to town while I ponder the volleyed conversational challenges of Muriel Goldblatt. My golden coat, my mauve chiffon trousers and tunic trimmed with baroque pearls, my jade and emerald necklace, they have all been dealt with by Muriel the iconoclast and I call her that, in my own mind, because her beliefs ultimately oppose all mine. If I were back in my pink house, with the towers of the City Palace on a hilltop to the east of my own garden where Persian roses grew, I would be correctly dressed and jewelled and Muriel Goldblatt would be considered the frump amongst espiocrats there. Every detail of her appearance would be reported back to the palace by the network of staff and their relatives that populated my small estate like a gang of spies, and Muriel would be found to be sadly lacking.

The Goldblatts' place is on a hilltop overlooking Hillingdon — I told you in the beginning that Hillingdon is not called Hillingdon for nothing — and on the journey back to my mother's house the landscape unfolds. We take the main road into town, the route from the north, and we pass an avenue of felled trees that would once have masked factories from the highway. They like cutting trees down in Hillingdon, I think, as the taxi skims along. We turn left by the old clocktower and take the hill, the car swooping. The library where I once worked erupts like a giant eye-tooth five doors away from the monumental front molar of the clocktower. Hillingdon is a town that always makes me think of teeth and their attrition. Gnawing worry. Sharp regret. The bite of grief. The mastication of many jaws over family *histoires*, including my own. The gluttony of scandals.

The library has new curtains. They used to be blue and now they are pink. Perhaps green and scarlet have been given a turn in my absence. I have been away for twenty years, after all. Mrs McPherson's cherry tree is still in the middle of her front lawn but I left a sapling and now there is a giant. A mansion on an irregular dog's-leg of land by the river is now occupied by a family. Children are playing on the lawn. There are toys on the terrace, laughter in the treetops, washing on the line, a line of little pants hanging on a tree. One of my mother's friends lived there and no one dropped a crumb at her bridge parties. I go home to my elephant smiling now, because things are different. People may scream on the stairs, cook in the kitchen, shout in the dining-room, splash in the bath in that house. My mother's friend is probably dead. My mother is definitely dead but there is life for the rest of us, and we are living it.

The house smells, faintly, of hot dust when I open the front door. The taxi driver has left me at the gate, far away through the trees, but he has waited there till I reach the front door. The house has a dark and shuttered look from the street, the windows still covered with boxes giving it a blinded look like that of a leper seeking alms.

"Spooky old place," he said, as he took the money for the fare, and he gave the property a careful look even though it was only midday on a sunny week day with an innocent little ship moored out in the harbour far below us. "They say—" he began, but I just said, "Yes, yes." I handed him the money and went away down the drive, through all the weeds and the creeping convolvulus and the wandering jew, because I did not wish to be told what any of them said. I knew it already. They say it is haunted and that my mother was mad, my father was mean, that I am mad as well and that the house is filthy, the garden rank.

The house smells of musty packing, of old newspapers, a faint tinge of mould on rainy days. It no longer smells of mice because the mice died silently and drily when they had eaten the blue pellets, and their bodies, when I find them, are as transparent as old oilcloth, tiny as dead butterflies. The birds in the roof were a different matter. Upstairs there is the lingering odour of death and decay because I had to fumigate the ceiling. I am very sorry about the decimation of the mice and the eviction of the starlings and sparrows from their labyrinths of straw, my mother's hair-combings and old shredded Mintie wrappers all mingled with fluff from what was left of the carpet. Some birds flew away, some did not. I have fumigated the ceiling again, this time to get rid of the ants and the flies that gathered over the feathered feast. It was them, or me, so it had to be them.

The holy man said it was useless to cry, that the expenditure of such moisture from the body will endanger its chances of life. But the holy man was originally one of the northern desert people and went to Agra to study in his late youth. I think he remained there out of habit and acceptance but the people from the deserts measure water, and the possession of it, in archaic and grandiloquent language to describe the arabesques of survival. So it was with the holy man. I do not cry, standing in the entrance hall with the front door slammed behind me, the taxi driver on his way back to town with his tales untold, the smell of dead flesh growing stronger as I go up the stairs. If you had seen me you would have thought me a grim woman with no feelings. The truth of the matter is that I am only a human being trying to survive.

But there is the sound of ringing so I go downstairs again, to the telephone at the end of its long cord that is the length of a hundred rodent tails.

"Hello?"

"Margaret." I recognise, immediately, the gusty voice of Muriel Goldblatt. "Margaret, I'm terribly bewildered. I lent you my nice Parker and I gave you my glasses and everything, and you haven't signed this thing for Barry." So Muriel is quicker off the mark than I thought she would be.

"No. I couldn't see it properly, you see, Muriel." There is a ridiculous irony in this. Muriel does not laugh and my own faint titter fades.

"What am I going to tell him when he comes home for lunch? He's going to be furious."

"You could tell him about your terracotta pots and all that lobelia and stuff. I thought it sounded really interesting." There is a long silence. "Hello? Muriel? Muriel, are you there?" But Muriel has gone.

CHAPTER FIVE

IN INDIA I was considered beautiful. You may be surprised
at that. My pale hair has always grown in angel curls. It was
plaited when I was a child, to keep it out of the way, my
mother said. I was always ashamed of my hair until I went to
India. There it was considered lovely and the simple people in
the markets and the streets invented a story that I was a
changeling who had been brought down to that desert city
from the northern hills. Yet I actually journeyed there from the
south, so many thousands of miles to the south that it would
have been beyond their comprehension, my journey there.

There is a legend in the area of a fair-haired people, with
wheaten-coloured skin and eyes as dark as pansies, who
come down from the hills when the season is auspicious and
the moon is in the right quarter. They are considered to have
magical qualities and to see them is an augury of good fortune, to hear their voices akin to listening to the songs of
benevolent sirens. So the ordinary people of the city considered me both lucky and beautiful and the crowds would part
for me when I walked in the streets.

The merchants and the more important shopkeepers
knew differently, though. They sometimes went down to
Delhi to do deals and gossip with other traders and hucksters
and to boast about themselves and their relatives, the beauty
of their wives, their fertility.

The big dealers and traders in Delhi knew that I arrived,
wearing a grimy pink coat, on an aeroplane from Singapore
and that they had been instructed to have samples of silks
and oils, bouquets of flowers awaiting me. I was met by

Ranji's nephew and taken to what was then the best hotel. It is all different now. Everything is different now. At that time the family no longer had a townhouse in Delhi. It went, together with a lot of other things, with Independence in 1947. Delhi was different too, so perhaps they might not have wanted to go there so much. I never asked about it. It might have made them sad, might have made Ranji melancholy. I developed a habit of not asking questions. The answers often do not matter. The answers would not have altered how I thought or felt, and there is a strength in reticence, a kind of dignity and separateness which was essential to me there.

Girls were waiting for me at the hotel. They wore gauzy trousers and jewelled tunics and I thought they looked like a flock of bright butterflies. I felt clumsy and dirty. I *was* clumsy and dirty. The journey had been a long one. I was very tired. Travel was more difficult then and everything took longer when you went from one place to another. I had made my way across the world starting off with a battle through the eye of a hurricane.

The girls bathed me in rose water and washed my pale hair in blue mud. They dyed my fingernails pearly bronze with henna paste and with that paste also made designs of roses and turrets, heraldic animals and amuletic devices for luck on my feet and my hands. I became unrecognisable and walked in handmade sandals tied with agate beads, my feet patterned with an embroidery of henna dye, my palms stained in patterns so that, later, when I leaned out my upper windows to wave goodbye to Ranji in the dawn, he would see roses ornamenting my hands and garlands of lilies up my arms. On feast days, when I was settled in my pink house in the north, we lit lamps and placed them in the old stone sconces at either side of the gates that led to my garden, and in this picturesque manner I lived for many seas—. But I am interrupted in this train of thought by the telephone.

"Hello? Is that," and here the speaker rustles about amongst papers, scrabbles on a desk for notes, "Miss Margaret Harris? Of 25 Hillingdon Avenue?"

I have to ponder this for a moment or two. There is a great disparity in how I am perceived, depending on location.

When I was painted with henna, clad in gauze, and lived in a land that should have been (but was not) foreign to me I was considered a beauty and an advantage to know. Now that I am back in what should be my own territory I am merely a nuisance. The voice contains impatience, and dismissal.

"Miss Margaret Harris, sole beneficiary in the estate of Ivy Evelyn Harris, widow, deceased, formerly resident at that address? 25 Hillingdon Avenue?"

I know who it is now. I know who owns this thin and superior tone that pokes into my ear like a finger, faintly derisory and derogatory. It is Daphne, the girl in the expensive Gucci loafers who pads round Goldblatt's office bringing him coffee with cream, with or without bagels and often at the wrong time.

"Yes." My own voice is very measured, slightly gritty as some little mechanism might be after many days without oil or fuel. And I have not been fuelled lately by admiration or charm, beauty or comfort, ease of thought or respect. Even the sound I make has been whittled away. "This is me," I say. This is the truth of the matter. Margaret Harris ceased to exist a long time ago, if not on the pavement outside the main doors of Kirkcaldie and Stains then certainly when that other voice, that ancient echo of long ago when I wanted an A for my Brontë essay, whispered in her ear, "Not now, Margaret, not now," and the receiver was plonked down to the tune of children's laughter.

"Miss Harris," the voice is admonitory now, "Mr Goldblatt has asked me to ring you to say he can't see you this week. Mr Goldblatt is far too busy this week to keep your usual appointment on Wednesday. Apart from being out of town on that day he says there's nothing to report yet due to the fact that a most essential paper hasn't been signed and until it's been signed nothing more can be done. We can proceed no further," she says, "until we have a signature."

"Oh." So I am in disgrace at Goldblatt's office, am I?

"If you'd like to pop in when you're passing, Miss Harris, I could attend to the matter for you. It wouldn't take a minute. Otherwise we'll just have to be in touch next week to let you know what's happening. Progress will be much slower without the signature but, as I've just said, we'll let you know what's happening."

"Or what's not happening." But she has gone, her own click of the receiver so much less emphatic than the professor's. My unfinished essay on finite element analysis of incomprehensible material within the literary framework of the Brontës must be somewhere in this disturbed house, somewhere amongst the walls of crates, the piles of boxes and the bags of rubbish. My own unfinished thoughts about everything, including myself and my own life and why I am here, are neatly filed in my own head, in alphabetical order. Hillingdon is not called Hillingdon for nothing — I have already told you that — but I was not a librarian for nothing either. So I have my own inner alphabet. A for — we'll forget A. For me, it is not a letter of the alphabet that has charm. B for Benares and bazaar. C for chattri, which is another word for tomb so my private alphabet is economical. I have done T as well. S for signature, and this puzzles me because I signed a lot of papers about my mother's estate when I first got back, so why is it so urgent that I sign an extra one now?

At night I sleep softly and lightly, like a child who has learnt her letters, on the little truckle bed I have placed on the landing upstairs and sometimes I watch the passage of the moonlight across the walls. It shines through the old balustrades, fanning the shadowed staircase like fingers held out to guard me.

Wallace is lodged in the old car shed at night but sometimes wanders out on to the seaward lawn when the moon swings high in the sky. In my sleep I hear the sound of the chain that links his front feet but he wears this fetter like a king, with pride as if it is a sign of office, and in the moonlight he surveys the garden. It might be an *arrondissement* to which he has restored order. And he has. I must say that. The very presence of the elephant in my garden has caused peace to fall on the shrubberies, on the overgrown lawns, on the actual air. Even the atmosphere remains, now, innocent and inviolate, with no more shouting from The Arsehole. *Bloody rich woman in your great big bloody house.* We do not hear that now. The sawdust from The Arsehole's tree-felling is washing into the soil, the scars on the garden are growing less noticeable. Ivy is beginning to grow over the stumps. The peace, though, is an uneasy one in which I do not completely believe. Only the elephant guards me with care. The others involved in this melodrama do not have my respect or trust. Even Goldblatt comes and goes in the realm of loyalty. My father would say Goldblatt blew with the wind, this way and that, depending on which was the most popular course and which would be most gainful for him.

"And how are you going with that elephant, Margaret?" Goldblatt is on the telephone again. "By the way, I'm sorry I can't see you this week but possibly I might have something to report next week. Without that signature, Margaret, our progress is very slow." He sighs. "One must just battle on, I daresay."

"I daresay." My voice is quite neutral. A beige voice, anonymous, like that of a funeral director who is accustomed to discussing the unthinkable.

"Anyway, Margaret, I just thought I'd better give you a little tinkle to enquire about the livestock." Goldblatt finds this very funny and it is a while before he can speak again. "My wife says you're getting a very colourful reputation round the town. Rumours of your lunacy abound, if I may say so, but we're stalwartly battling away on your behalf. Only yesterday I heard Muriel on the telephone chatting away to someone and I distinctly heard her say, "No, you're quite wrong there. Margaret Harris is definitely not loony. She is just very unusual.'"

"It isn't my fault." My voice is sharp now. I can see why Goldblatt, in one of our earlier interviews, looked at me in an assessing kind of way and said, "I'm not sure what the future holds for you, Margaret. I'm not sure anyone would be willing to take you on. I do hope you realise that you face a very grim future? If you made an effort to tone yourself down you might meet someone. You might marry again." Goldblatt was triumphant about this. "A professional man. Perhaps an accountant. Someone who could keep an eye on things for you, Margaret. Someone who could look after you." His voice became as expansive and well-upholstered as a large double eiderdown with real feathers.

"But it wouldn't be possible for me to marry again, Goldblatt."

"I fully realise it takes a while to forget the past, Margaret. But if you made an effort, if you wore a nice frock, for instance, instead of those—" He gestured towards my tunic and trousers. I think I might have been in blue and silver that day with ankle chains of lapis lazuli mounted in platinum.

"It wouldn't ever be possible for me to marry again, Goldie, because I've never been married in the first place." Goldblatt put his head in his hands. I may be one of the most innocently difficult clients Goldblatt has ever had.

"The fact that there's an elephant in your garden is causing a bit of talk in the neighbourhood," says Goldblatt now, "but I've done my best to scotch all the rumours because, in part, I feel somewhat to blame for the situation you're in up there. I did say to you that I'd ask my brother about a guard dog and we've really just gone on, innocently enough, from there. I think," says Goldblatt, "that people are beginning to understand, and it isn't as if it's going to be forever. In a week or so, certainly not any more than a fortnight, we'll have to get him on the train and send him back to where he comes from. My brother's had word from Prawar Brothers and it seems they've got themselves in order and they'll be sending for him. They say the grand parade isn't the same without him. Sadly," says Goldblatt, "as far as I can gather, the only goods train that runs from here to Wellington comes through about dawn so it'll be an early start for you. Perhaps we could find someone to help. I could have a word with my brother's wife; she was one of the Baileys. I'm sure you'll remember the Baileys? Great big family of boys? Lived in that enormous house up by the racecourse? Loaded with money going way back? She's got six brothers and they've all got three or four sons apiece. Perhaps I could prevail upon some of them to help. They've already been awfully good about it all. They're related to the Mayor, by marriage, and also the Town Clerk, as I understand it, so dispensations to keep a large animal in your backyard haven't been a problem. It's just been a teeny weeny matter of having the right little word in the right little ear over dinner, Margaret. You'll remember, I'm sure, that old Hillingdon saying: the Goldblatts talk to the Baileys and the Baileys talk to the Prendergasts and the Prendergasts talk to God?" Goldblatt is in a talkative mood today. "We've got a Prendergast in as Mayor at the moment and the Town Clerk's mother was née Prendergast, if you're still following me, Margaret, and you yourself are vaguely related to the Prendergasts and the Baileys through marriage on your mother's side of the family so don't despair about getting that bloody elephant to the station." We are both silent at the thought of marching through the streets of Hillingdon to the railway station before dawn, leading Wallace at the end of a piece of cord, which, to the theatrical and the gossip-hungry, would seem to be hardly more than a bit of string. Dawn, I think. Dawn. A sad time of day when the heart oftens sinks about what might lie ahead before noon.

Netta got me up at dawn the day I left my house of carnation-coloured stone with its secret gardens of roses and verbena. The sky was pink to match the marble colonnades outside my doors, and Netta laid out the cards on the floor of my bedroom for the very last time, garlands of Spades and Hearts in circles giving out their messages of luck, their omens of ill fortune. I don't believe it, of course. I've never believed it. She had already read the clouds by then and the news was not auspicious. She did not tell me this but I saw her turn to every point on the compass, gazing up at the day's new sky, and then she said nothing. If it had been good fortune thus forecast she would have told me. So I knew the signs were bad. Dark clouds had gathered over the hills to the north, from whence came the lucky changeling folk in times long past, even I could read that well enough. And the view of the desert to the south was blurred that morning by wind devils.

Netta sat cross-legged on the marble floor and laid out the cards. Three times she did it, she cast the cards upon that bold beautiful floor with its checkerboard of pink and black squares and three times the answer was the same. I supposed she was anxious about me. She wanted to send me away with a lightness of heart, with the thought that I was merely travelling from one place of beauty and tranquillity to another, death only a minor interruption to my progress. I think she wanted me to go away believing that one day I would remember that place as just a location where I lived once, a long time ago. And that the death that made us close the shutters so there were rooms never touched by a sight of day since then, that death would just be a sad thing that happened a long time ago as well. I think she sought to make it transitory, inconsequential, merely a tiny part of a better whole to which I could look forward. Not so.

Three times she laid out the circular form of cards, the garland known as the Lucky Thirteen and thrice the nine of Spades was at the heart. The first time she took the middle card, turned it over and saw what it was she said, "It is a mistake." The birds were beginning to sing in my trees by then and through the shutters came a bar of early sun, as wide as a stick for flogging. The day would be a long one. I had far to go. I say my trees, but they were not mine, were never mine though for many years the illusion had existed in my mind that they were.

Netta shuffled the pack and laid out the garland again. When she turned the cards to read the omens there was the nine of Spades again, at the heart of the circle, the unluckiest card in the world.

Netta had a book about the cards. The old princess gave it to her one summer when she was sent all the way to Nice to be a companion for a season, till they got a suitable nurse. In Nice there was little to do for an old princess anchored by arthritis, who no longer goes to the casino and whose friends and lovers are all dead long ago. Great-aunt of a maharaja. Recipient of bank orders and statements that lumbered through the laborious monetary system at the City Palace, but never a letter from anyone, never a genuine personal enquiry. She had been pensioned off because she had outlived her time, and now I am pensioned off for the same reason, but I am younger and nobody's great-aunt. Even her telephone hardly ever rang except for the concierge to say there was no mail again. So the old princess was deeply into omens and luck. Netta once told me she even had a private soothsayer, a Turk, who during the day had a café and in the evenings sometimes did the rounds of disenfranchised ancient royalty, for a fee, telling the tarot cards and laying out an ordinary pack into the Lucky Thirteen to get a reading on, possibly, an enthroned future. Or, in a smaller way, a better price than expected when they sold the final necklace, the last diadem, the definitive bracelet to the breakers. Many of them were no longer ambitious. Perhaps they might have been glad to hear that the omens foresaw them sitting on a slightly bigger balcony with a tiny glimpse of the sea. The Turk catered for all that and would sell them, at a reduced rate, little leftover boxes of Turkish Delight from his shop if the news was bad. The sweetmeats were dusty with icing sugar fine as the ground bones of ortolans.

Netta used to say that ordinary cards were, in their own way, as accurate as the tarot pack but gave a meatier, grittier reading of the world. Three times she laid out the Lucky Thirteen and three times the first card she turned over was the nine of Spades. You cannot argue with that. It is the worst card in the pack. Even coupled with the best of cards its ill-luck is never diminished. Poverty, misery, death: that is what the nine of Spades means. Three times in a row it had come up, so we both knew that it was my card. She gave up then, because it was useless. We already knew about death and destruction, because it had occurred. The ashes of the pyre were probably still warm then, and by noon I would have long gone so it was not only the death of a man. It was the demise of life as I had known it. The book said so, the old princess's book about the meaning of cards, and it was true.

The Turk taught Netta the rudiments of the skill, though we did not have a tarot pack, just an ordinary one and sometimes I used to play Patience with it when Ranji stayed away too long.

The dawn came up very rosy the day I left as if the sky bloomed one last time for me. Dead leaves were rustling on the terraces, blown along by an ill little wind, when the car arrived to take me to Delhi. They made a scratchy noise akin to that made by the husks of mice beneath my mops and brushes now.

"The car is here." Old Gopal's voice at the door sounded like a last bell.

Netta looked out the window, through the carved marble lattice that screened us from the day.

"The car is here," she said, so I believed it then. Gopal was an old man. His eyesight was poor. It was possible he had been mistaken. "I hope it is not the captain," she said. Then she looked through the lattice again. "It is the captain." So we both knew what to expect. The captain was a silent man and we both construed his muteness as contempt. He may have been shy but his hush was always deathly and almost enduring. He would sometimes say a word or two but his austerity passed for disdain even amongst Indians. The only time I ever went to the City Palace I saw two women running down one of the inner ramps ahead of me on my way out. "Captain Kothari," they said. "Captain Kothari." And they disappeared into a room, the slam of whose door still echoed as he called to me from an upper landing, "Have you seen two women?"

"No," I said. "I am here alone but, if you wish, we could walk together back to the car." We went in silence and I felt ill at ease.

"It is Captain Kothari," said Netta that day I left, and we went out slowly to the car, which was the big silver Austin Ranji always liked so much. It was used for picnics because it was spacious, a glorious relic of ancient motoring so well looked after that the interior never quite lost the scent of new hide. The upholstery was burgundy-coloured leather and I suppose someone had the job of polishing it regularly or, otherwise, why would it always smell new?

Captain Kothari was standing by the driver's door, just waiting, a neat tailored figure in a blue linen suit. The blue a little sharp for my taste but the captain was one to linger on the senses. In the bazaar some said his grandfather was once an executioner and others claimed he came from a distant village where his father, the headman, had taken the land of widows and orphans and thus made himself rich. All this could have been just gossip. The bazaar was always full of gossip, most of it ill-founded but some of it charming. For example, as I have told you, they always said I was one of the magic changelings from the northern mountains. Netta told me once that Captain Kothari had been brought up in the orphanage under the city walls and that his shyness and reticence were deep and penetrating. Even as a baby, she said, he never cried. The holy man from Agra told me a long time ago that only an ignorant man becomes angry, the wise man understands everything. So I understood that there was much about Captain Kothari I did not comprehend, and I stepped into the Austin without speaking a word. If I had greeted him he may not have answered and as I, that morning, luxuriated in silent distress no more of it could be provoked.

Captain Kothari held the back door of the car open. I stepped inside and I kept the palms of my hands flattened against the discs on the front of my golden coat because I did not wish the captain to hear the sound of my fortune. I was sure he knew what I was doing, what we had done, because he gave me one of his veiled glances just quickly like a sharp aside in conversation, a penetrating remark from a herald. The only sound for many miles on the first leg of the journey was the faint tinkle of the golden sequins Netta had sewn to my jacket. Stamped or engraved with lucky runes by the old goldsmith from the market, it rustled every time I moved and I did move from time to time even though I was aware that when I did so the captain glanced at me in the rear vision mirror.

In my own mind I said goodbye to the streets and the buildings and the animals, I said goodbye to the fields of hay and the camels that pulled the carts, and I sometimes abandoned my infinite stillness to raise my hand in one last greeting to strangers who bent to stare in the windows of the car when we were delayed by traffic in the inner city. So I left the place where I had lived for so long and as I went southward again I sometimes looked at the magic signs the smith had put on my sequins. The sign of a castle on a hill, for power. The rising sun over the sea, for aggression. The scales, for balance. The artist's palette, for expression. The pyramids, for steadiness. An open book, for mystery. The star, for adventure. A rainbow, for dependability. The smith had given me a fortune in lucky wishes sewn into my coat, but bereft of joy and without hope I travelled south in silence.

The first teahouse in the desert was three hours out from the city, a morning's journey from my house and my life. The place was nearly filled by a party of tourists from a bus, but Captain Kothari ushered me through the crowd, still in silence. He was not a rude man. His gestures were courteous enough. But his silence was so enduring, his lack of warmth seemed so stalwart, that it could pass for discourtesy. In the teahouse leaves had fallen from a tree beside the terrace and they rattled like little finger bones reaching under chairs and when people moved those chairs that sounded, to me, like screaming. But I was not well by then. I was ill from fear and anguish, and this would have coloured my thoughts. The people there, the people who had come off the bus, were busy talking about what they had seen. They were English, touring after a conference in Delhi. Agra, the Taj Mahal, what the managing director had thought of it, snake charmers, who had the runs today, what photographs they had taken to show the family back home. I sat there in a dream and listened to it without hearing it properly.

"Tea," said the captain and put the cup and saucer in front of me on a small table. So that was one word I had wrenched out of him. *This is us at some teahouse in the desert.* I could imagine what the people from the bus would say when they had the films developed. *We stopped there one day for a rest. Yes, it was just like a miniature palace, just plonked right down in the middle of nowhere. Arthur was really upset, weren't you Arthur, because he was feeling a little bit better by then and he said he thought he might be able to manage a scone, or even a little sandwich, just a little something to fill up the gap and there wasn't a thing to eat, not a thing, just the tea. They only served tea. The lady on the left? Oh, we never knew who she was. Very mysterious, Arthur said. Loves his little joke, does Arthur. Blonde she was. Dressed in Indian clothes as if she'd worn them all her life but you could tell she was English. All right, Arthur. You're always correcting me. Arthur says he said she was European. He thought she might be French. Yes, I know you can speak for yourself, Arthur. I'm just telling the story my way. If you look at this shot of us all holding up our cups and saying "Cheese" you can see her again, closer. Myra said, didn't you Myra, "Imagine wearing earrings*

*that size at this hour of the day." And the managing director —
that's him there, that fattish man with the hat on — he said his
father was a jeweller and, unless he was very much mistaken, they
were real, those stones. We said "Hello" to her, just out of devil-
ment, but she didn't answer, just climbed in a big silver car with a
funny little fellow and they drove away. They went south, back the
way we'd come. Yes, I know Arthur looks as if he's pulling a silly
face. He was in one of his moods that day and when we all said,
"Cheese," he said, "Bugger."*

As we drew away from the teahouse, when the captain
changed from second to third gear, I said to him, "I know
how you could make a fortune." I knew there would be no
answer. I leaned forward and placed my elbows on the back
of his seat, an ultimate and insolent invasion of his space.
"You could have a nice big oven installed in that place back
there and you could set up an industry making scones for
tourists."

"All I want to do," said the captain, "is get us on our way
as quickly as possible," and he changed swiftly from fourth
to overdrive. But he said the word 'us'. So I was content with
that. All I want to do is get us on our way as quickly as possible. For the captain, such a remark might pass as a faint concession. I sat back, with one of my hands on my bag. Netta
had packed hardly anything for me, so the weight and mag-
nitude of my baggage might attract no attention. My packing
was akin to flaked and dehydrated food, which the addition
of water would swell to five times the size. It was like the
heart of an elephant, the pupil of a golden eye, the soul of a
fox.

"I think we'd better get on our way," said the captain as
we left the teahouse far behind us. "We must be in Agra as
early as possible."

Netta had a bag made for me to take away, a kind of
Gladstone bag made of Indian carpet of the finest weave, and
in it she had packed my silk clothes all rolled up with the
jewelcase at the very centre. The silver thread and the golden
tinselled trappings of the tunics, the pearl fastenings, were all
genuine. I would be able to sell them, by weight and size,
later if I wished. I sat with one hand on this miniature and

disguised bank vault and the other on my golden runes as I added up the total of the captain's words. All I want to do is get us on our way as quickly as possible = 15 words. I think we'd better get on our way = 8 words. We must be in Agra as early as possible = 9 words. A total of 32.

One of the tourists had said, "Just look at that hair," when I climbed in the car again. Netta had painted my hairline with red ochre in the old style that village women still favour for days of note like weddings and feasts and funerals, so decked like an old bride I was being sent away.

"We must hurry," said Captain Kothari, and I added this to the total as I saw hawks faltering in the updraughts of warm air from the desert. The hills of the city were away to the north now and the dust in suspension made the air a golden mystery with no horizons. 32 plus 3 = 35 words, a world record for conversations with Captain Kothari. But I had forgotten the word 'tea' and remembered it only much later when we had crossed the desert and had gone through a border between one state and another. The soldiers had guns, but they waved us on as soon as the car approached the checkpoint. I suppose someone had telephoned ahead to say we were coming. One of them bent down and looked through the window of the car at me and his face was solemn and dark with something, perhaps regret. It was not an unkind look. I was very thirsty by then. Tea. I thought of the tea we had had back in the desert. That made 36 words. And much later, days later, when I began to walk out to the aeroplane, out over the melting tarmac, Captain Kothari called after me, "I do not think the lady should have spoken about your hair in that manner, the lady at the teahouse. Your hair," said Captain Kothari, "is very beautiful." So that was an extra 25 words that I forgot completely till many weeks later.

Chapter Six

MY DEAR FRIEND Miss Margaret Harris, I hope this letter finds you hale and hearty.

A letter has arrived for me, from India. The envelope is made from beige parchment like the whisper of dried leaves, painted in the lefthand corner with a bunch of roses. The notepaper matches exactly. It is handmade, chosen or manufactured with care. The stamps are royal purple and the ink that forms the copperplate letters is golden. When I saw this message lying amongst dead leaves and dust in the old letterbox I trembled. It was so beautiful I imagined I picked it, like a peach. It is such a long time since I received a letter, since I heard from anyone.

It is very sad that our Maharaja has passed away and I would never be able to see him again and wait outside in the car hearing your laughter so pretty. Who can have sent me this message, I wonder? *Our Maharaja was indeed a kind and generous man and that is why we will always remember him, and you. A new hope rests with the estate of the mother and father of the beloved Miss Harris. It is very sad that they are passing away, but in time to take care of the daughter, our aforementioned beloved Miss Harris. I pray for their peace in Heaven and wish you a New Year with some good news. Please drop me a line or two to let me know if I can be of some use. I have a cousin in business not a great distance as the crow flies from the home of your late mother and father. Many years ago he was most happy to render a favour to you about a motorcar but you were, of course, not knowing him personally at the time. My cousin has since been blessed with a beautiful wife and three handsome sons. Two are now lawyers and the youngest is an accountant, all in the best firms. With kindest admiration and regards, Yours very, very sincerely, Gulab Kothari.*

I am silenced for the rest of the day and continue to unpack boxes and crates, stupified by this news. From time to time I return to the letter, which I have propped up in the middle of the mantelpiece, to re-read these startling and magical words. So it was Gulab Kothari's cousin who returned the eau-de-Nil Cortina to my father, to this very house. Gulab Kothari's cousin must be the Indian fruiterer in the distant seaport I made for on the night of the storm. He must have left his shop, collected the car from where I had left it parked at the port, slewed halfway across a yellow line in a parking area marked *Harbour Master Only*. Then there would have been the endless drive back to Hillingdon through the night, easing through the end of the cyclone. It must have been Gulab Kothari's cousin who did that for me.

Later the same day another note appears in the letterbox, thrust in this time by grimy fingers which have left their marks upon the paper. The paper itself is just a sheet torn from an exercise book and the writing is large, masculine and aggressively careless, going this way and that as if the writer is a man of many moods and all of them unpredictable.

Dear Resident of 25 Hillingdon Avenue, A word to let you know that we will be taking over our land and building on Saturday, ample warning having been given to clean up mess in same and if finding rubbish still in position complaints to be registered re mess with the Health Department (rodent threat etc). Also with regard to large animal kept without restraint in backyard and no sanitation (fly nuisance) complaint already registered with Health Department pending investigation. Yours sincerely. This is followed by an indecipherable signature.

"Could I please speak to Mr Goldblatt urgently?" I am on the telephone again to Goldblatt's office. Outside the cicadas are screaming that summer is ending, the sun has an odd pinkish cast because a bushfire on the edge of town has filled the sky with smoke and the light from flames, and around my feet lie large plastic buckets whose lids are firmly closed with old Sellotape that is lifting at the edges. Mother must have attended to security, within the realm of possibility.

"How are you, Miss Harris?" So Daphne now recognises my voice on the telephone. "What may I do for you today? I'm afraid Mr Goldblatt's still away in Sydney. He won't be back till late on Friday. Is there something I could do for you in the meantime, or will you wait till then?"

"I didn't realise Goldie, I mean Mr Goldblatt, was that far away. I just thought he might be busy with meetings or something like that." I stir uneasily in the old larder and one foot knocks over a bucket from which necklaces spill. Suddenly there is a rainbow on the floor: chains and ropes of improbably large pink and blue pearls, a massive brass heart locket, silver rings, the glint of a giant topaz. This is what Goldblatt has been going on about, what he has been waiting for.

"Are you all right, Miss Harris? I thought I heard you give a gasp, as if you got a fright. Miss Harris? Are you there?"

I have dropped to my hands and knees before the treasure. Right down the bottom of what is left in the bucket I see the glimmer of gold brooches and something that could be a handful of these sovereigns Goldblatt has nagged about.

"I'm so sorry to be inattentive." I have returned to the telephone, to the inestimable Daphne who will repeat to Goldblatt every word I say so it is suddenly essential that she is presented with an innocent blandness. I do not want Goldblatt to find out what I have discovered in Mother's wall of buckets that hides the entrance to the sunroom upstairs. It was once my bedroom. As I stir the pile with one foot I see a diamond ring set with three large stones surface, blazing, beside an Art Deco bracelet that may be gold and slightly to the left is a string of lapis lazuli beads. The clasp looks as if it might be set with a cabochon sapphire.

"I just got a slight fright because a bee flew in through the window and I'm very allergic to their stings. I'm so sorry to be inattentive, Daphne." This is an instantaneous prevarication. If Goldblatt finds out about my discovery he will want the stuff put in his safe and I'm not sure this is what I require. "I wanted to speak to Mr Goldblatt because I've received a message from that neighbour of mine who keeps cutting trees down for firewood. He hasn't been in here for a couple of weeks, not since I got the elephant, but this note he's left in my letterbox says he'll be claiming my shed and all the land between my shed and the boundary this Saturday. And he also says he's complained to the Health Department about Wallace being here — about the elephant — and Mr Goldblatt told me he'd had a word with the Mayor about all that. It was all taken care of, he said. And now I don't know what to do, Daphne. I don't know what to do." My voice rises to a wail as I stand ankle-deep in some of Mother's more specialised shopping, my feet suddenly bound together by a string of pearls with an elaborate clasp set with coloured stones. Wallace, when he patrols the seaward lawn in the moonlight, drags his ankle chains to make a clinking noise. I emulate this as I talk to Daphne, but in miniature as if I am a tiny statue of an elephant in the temple of my mother's house, a small figurine depicting the elephant god Ganesi.

"I can hear a funny little noise," says Daphne. "Are you quite sure you're all right, Miss Harris?"

"I'm fine, Daphne. I just tripped over something, that's all."

"Well, all I can do," says Daphne, "is give Mr Goldblatt your message when he rings in from where he's staying." She seems to be shuffling through more papers on her desk. "I've got an emergency number where I can ring him if necessary. He usually telephones in the morning to see if there's anything urgent happening and I've got this emergency number I can ring if it's absolutely necessary but he doesn't like me to do that unless it's something really shattering." There is more noise of papers being moved about. "Here it is." Daphne is triumphant. "Thorpy. That's the name. Chez Thorpy. He's left it written here. Oh, dear." There is a long silence. "I've just read a note on the bottom. He's written here that on no account is this to be divulged to anyone. Oh, Miss Harris—"

"It's quite all right." My voice is very measured now. I am back to the sepulchral funeral director's tone now, gritty and very beige. "I won't tell a soul, Daphne. Just tell him about The Ar — about that man when he telephones in the morning and we'll leave it like that for the moment. It's a while till Saturday, anyway." I am comforting Daphne now and I am the person in need of solace and reassurance. The holy man from Agra said that a pure and strong will is all powerful but I doubt if my willing The Arsehole to clear off will keep him away. "We've got a few days till Saturday and a lot can happen in that length of time, Daphne. Don't worry." I ring off and sink down on to the pile of pearls and coins. So Goldblatt is involved with Gloria Thorpy. And that's why he knew all about her house and her legs and the colour of her eyes and a lot more besides.

"My God!" I shout in Mother's mousy residence and my voice echoes through the rooms, up the stairwell, as far as the barrier of buckets that bars my way to my old bedroom. "My God, my God!" And Wallace comes to the pantry window and puts his trunk through the aperture as if we are both Hindus making offerings of appeal and supplication, succour and comfort within the framework of an obscure shrine devoted to the sins of Goldblatt. "Oh, my God, my God!" Wallace takes the receiver from my hand and replaces it on the hook.

Outside there is a faint smell of burning. The neighbourhood is a neat and orderly one. People have aspirations towards tidiness, and status deriving from that tidiness, up here on the hill in Hillingdon. There is a plaque on a lamppost near my mother's house and it says 'Tidiest Street Of The Year' followed by a blurred date that is unreadable. Residents are raking autumn leaves from their lawns, cutting the edges of the grass and they are having little bonfires of the rubbish because on the hill in Hillingdon rubbish is outlawed. The aromatic scent of burning gum leaves and scented grasses has a specialised charm like that of simple incense burnt in a temple when a farmer has died.

The people came down from the hills when Ranji died and they stripped the ridges and valleys of timber as they walked. They came to the pyre bearing wood so when the fire was lit it burned for three days and three nights, the flames so bright they were like the light in the iris of a god's eye. The land was laid waste for a hundred miles in every direction and sat beneath a sky filmed with smoke and ash. They had travelled in silence, the only sound was that of wagon wheels, the jingling of a camel's harness or the sound of cooking pots when the women prepared food. The season was a dry one. It is always dry in the north but when Ranji died it was a drier season than usual as though the weather bleached itself like bones. The rains had not yet come so the eye of the land gazed up at the golden sky, parched and languishing under the seduction of dolour.

He had been their maharaja since he was five and a half years old. I thought he would live forever. Perhaps the people also believed this because he had been their ruler as far back as they could remember, and back also into the time of their fathers. People do not have long lives in that part of the world. Their silence matched my own in a landscape made eerie by the creaking of a thousand carts, the circle of desolation extending to where the mountains rose in the north and the desert reached the holy man's railway to the south. I say the holy man's railway, but the holy man just lived in a hut of mud and straw beside the line. His decrees about the trains were always stunningly accurate, accepted by the local people, morbid with belief and curiosity, as edicts from the gods. I think the holy man was merely skilled at listening to the rails for the vibrations that meant a train was coming, but such things pass for magic or the knowledge imparted by an inner eye in those parts.

The day I was driven south by Gulab Kothari, to the airport in Delhi, I felt that the car was like a fly crawling over the eye of a corpse because the land had become dead, laid out under the sun like an unmeaty carcass. Even the carrion birds no longer wheeled and turned high in the sky that day I travelled with only the sound of those reluctant words to punctuate the time. But I am forgetting the last remark: 25 words, and all those about my golden hair, a piece of dialogue that puzzles me now that I have received the letter from India. *With kindest admiration and regards. Yours very very sincerely, Gulab Kothari.* The birds had also gone south that day, and for many days afterwards, to where fields were high with maize, where there was meat for the picking and sometimes a little shade.

On the shadowy landing upstairs in this shadowed house I sleep in the truckle bed and I dream of corpses. Never the

90

one on the pyre because I never saw it. Netta went out, just once, to find out what was happening, and we knew when the fires were lit because we saw the smoke rising. Then she closed the shutters and we saw no more but there was always the smell of burning. For days there was the smell of burning. I dream now of a body I once saw in the Jamuna River so perhaps it is water I crave, to put the fire out.

"Look at that," I said and I pointed down to the sluggish current than ran beneath the balustrading of the Taj Mahal. "I can see something tied down in the river," I said. "What's that down there, in the river. Is it a bundle of sticks?"

"Come away, my darling." Ranji, in those days, sometimes took me on expeditions to see the sights and I saw the Taj Mahal three or four times, but only once in the moonlight when it is at its best. It was a long time ago. After a while, I don't remember how long, we just stayed in the inner city. We played mah jong and walked in the garden and he had books sent from London for me, anything I liked. And that is how the years passed. We may have grown old, though I always thought of us both as young, and no longer felt the need to display ourselves.

"Come away, my darling," said Ranji again. "Come away."

Captain Kothari was with us that day, standing away at a distance because he was a kind of equerry, a sort of secretary, and was supposed to be there when he was needed and not there when discretion was required. It must have been a difficult brief to fill, I think now. Ranji shouted something to him in Hindi, I couldn't catch what it was, and the captain walked back along that slender lake in front of the building. He went towards the gatehouse where the great wooden doors had shut behind us the previous night with such a dull sound of finality that I became frightened. The Taj Mahal by moonlight. I was being shown the sights. But now it was daytime and the Taj was basking in a sun masked from us by clouds of pollution from factories. The Taj by sunlight. Our jaunt followed a prescribed and proscribed pattern, like that in a tourist brochure. Agra was then a polluted place — it may still be so — and I remember how my nostrils stung when I breathed. If I had been asked what I wanted I would have said I would rather stay at home, stay in my pink house, to read or listen to music.

"Come away," said Ranji but I stood there, leaning on the back balustrading far above the river, and I watched how the body drifted this way and that in the slow current, always tethered to its stake. It looked like a bundle of twigs and branches but such a bundle would not have knees and nor would it have a skull with bland eye sockets where the birds had fed. At night now I dream of a carcass in a river, of bones in the moonlight, a withered leg raised in convulsion or supplication, the claw of a hand above the water, a carrion bird perching on a thigh bone to gorge deeply on strips of flesh.

Upstairs in the moonlight, when I lie on the truckle bed trying to sleep, the shadows from the trees outside flicker on the floors and walls, and into my mind, flicker-flicker, come glimpses of things I thought I had forgotten. The corpse in the river and how the following day, when we returned, there were screens up so the body could not be seen. The market where Netta and I used to go shopping. Cumin seeds, cardamom, garam masala, asafoetida, turmeric. The merchants used to weigh out the spices, choose the best vegetables and fruit, wrap the soap that was made from goats' milk, and then there would be the beads flick-flacking on the thread with the tally. Green thread for the fruiterer. Red thread for the dealer in meat. Yellow for the goldsmith. Blue for the dealer in cloth. Someone from the palace — perhaps it was Captain Kothari — used to do the rounds of the merchants every week to pay them.

"Do you eat enough?" Ranji said to me once. "Do you have enough of everything? Are you happy? Is there anything you wish to buy and do not? The bills," he said, "are so very small, my darling. Is there anything you would like?"

"Books," I said. "Perhaps I might like some more books," so after that the catalogues came from the big bookstores in London and I would mark things I thought looked interesting. Parcels would arrive, many weeks later, and old Gopal used to come hopping in, using his hoe as a crutch because he had a withered foot.

"Many books containing much wisdom," he used to say, but they were only novels, only books about love and death and vanity. Love and death and vanity were the things that took me there, and love was what kept me in that place for so long. Death sent me on my way again. And vanity? I have given up vanity.

Vanity once took me to the City Palace, but only once and then at the very end of my time in India. When Ranji had died. When we were packing. When we had heard the rumours that the maharanee was also packing and would be going to live in a bungalow within the walled garden of an old palace on the outskirts of town. That was when I got the invitation, only at the very end, and I went out of vanity and curiosity and sadness because none of it mattered any more and I could, without horror, now regard the shards of my life. You can reach a stage sometimes when your flesh feels like straw in the wind and you can drift like a husk in a reaped field.

Netta said, "Oh madam!" when the invitation arrived. I had become 'madam' by then and Netta had begun to pack, so it was time to go.

Her Highness The Dowager Maharanee requests the pleasure of the company of Miss Margaret Harris at an At Home on Saturday the Nineteenth of November at the City Palace at 4 p.m. RSVP Regrets Only. Dress: Informal.

Captain Kothari came and collected me in one of the cars, a green Lanchester that day, and we drove through streets that were silent. I just sat there, sat in the back seat. I think he asked me once if I was all right, was I comfortable, something like that. Probably I said, "Yes." I can't remember it very well. I remember catching his eye a couple of times when he tilted the rear vision mirror to see me sitting there. I thought he did not like me, probably despised me for living there for so long, but I wonder about it now when I think of his letter. *With kindest admiration and regards. Yours very, very sincerely.* I went through a side gate when I climbed out of the car. The captain had stopped at a small side entrance in the palace wall and when I approached the gate it opened as I stretched out my hand to the nob. There was a man in livery, in the palace's silk livery, standing on the other side, and when I set foot inside the wall the fountains began to play. It seemed magical to me but the staff have their spy holes and their little windows from which signals are given so my arrival must have been watched for and noted. They would have been waiting for me.

The captain took me through a web of stone paths and people were waiting to spread carpets as I walked, so my feet never touched rock or earth. Different servants preceded us when we went through the doors that opened on to the gardens from the lower floors of the eastern tower, and the rugs they spread out on the stone ramps that took us from one floor to another were blue and white. Those outside had been multi-coloured. Pink like roses. Blue as the sky. Green as moss. Yellow like the sun. Brown as the earth. The rugs they unrolled in front of me as I walked indoors were blue and white, a chilly checkerboard, and the air also struck cool but sweet after the heat outside.

We walked, the captain and I, up all the ramps that led to the top floor where the private apartments were. Apart from the people who unrolled the carpets as we walked, we saw nobody, but many would have seen us through the grilles and screens, through the peepholes and spyholes in the panelling. I have no doubt of that. So I kept myself very erect, expressionless, and I walked very straight and tall through the palace and never stopped for a moment or paused for breath. It would not have been a good thing to display any weakness to the watchers.

"Would you like to stop for a moment," said the captain when we reached the second landing, but I just shook my head and we passed on through to the third ramp. They do not have stairs in the royal buildings there. They have ramps because once the wives and the concubines were taken from floor to floor in little carriages pulled by servants, and on the stone ramps, at the side of the rugs, I saw the mark of many wheels ground into the rock. But I walked; and I walked swiftly, tall and plain in my manner like a woman from a farm who moves without guile. So we went up to the very top of the palace without ever resting though I would have liked to very much.

At the head of the third ramp I saw the maharanee standing in the shadows and, when I looked around, the captain and the men who had spread out the rugs for me to walk upon had all gone. They had disappeared into the shadowed recesses of that place without a sound, and without a sound I followed the maharanee along a corridor and into a sitting-room with a balcony that looked over an inner courtyard paved with stone. The sacred monkeys were playing on the columns and balustrades. No greeting was given to me and nor did I greet anyone. I followed in silence, out of pride and bewilderment because I did not know what else I could do. You can reach an end, and that was my finale.

The room had a vaulted ceiling and was larger than any in my house but small by palace standards. I suppose you could say that. It was an intimate room, a private room. Perhaps it was the maharanee's own private little sitting-room. There was a large desk in the middle of the floor, and it stood on a blue and white rug like those I had walked on earlier. That carpet was finer, though, the weave more dense, the shades of the colour like jewels. It might have been silk. The others were wool or cotton. And on the desk there were photographs in silver frames, paperweights that looked like crystal by Baccarat holding down letters written on royal blue paper and inscribed with the same golden ink I now have in Gulab Kothari's message. On the walls hung portraits of other earlier rulers in head-dresses of silk and pearls, emeralds on their breastplates and diamonds at their waists. And their women, there were paintings of their women, doe-eyed creatures with hair veiled in silk, the glimmer of precious stones through the gauzy draperies, nostrils pierced with gold and pearls. But none were like me, tall and guileless as a farmer's wife on an outing, wearing yellow muslin and earstuds of simple agate. I had gone there plainly dressed because by doing so I wished to state silently that I was not a menace, that I had no illusions about myself, that I did not think grandly and nor did I wish to impose myself anywhere. The language of clothing can be silent but very telling, as eloquent as a speech and perhaps more valuable because it can be assimilated at leisure.

Between the desk and the long doors that opened on to the balcony were two large rolled arm sofas, loose-covered in pale blue watered silk and facing each other like those you see in pictures of country houses in England. Ranji once told me that his wife had been brought up in England, that she had gone to school there and had many friends in London. Her mother had been an English model and caught another maharaja's eye when she did a fashion show for Hartnell at Claridge's. They were great ones, I always thought, to import women.

Sometimes — and I often wondered about this over the years — parcels of my books would arrive much more quickly than I supposed they would, and their arrival coincided with one of the maharanee's trips to London to see her friends. I used to wonder if, perhaps, the maharanee brought my books back with her, but I never asked. India is a place like that. It is a place where there are things you do not ask, and I never asked so that was, perhaps, part of my charm. It is not passivity. It is strength, for it takes great strength of mind and character to cast out curiosity and replace it with silent grace.

"Milk?" she said, and that was the first time I ever heard her voice. There was a teatray on a low table made of crystal and black glass and she began to pour tea into yellow porcelain cups, thin as a whisper. "Sugar? Do, please, sit down."

"Thank you." And that was the first time my voice was ever heard there as well. "I prefer my tea just plain," I said, "no milk and no sugar." And I sat down then, just plainly like a farm woman would on an outing where she knows she must behave well. I sat down on the sofa opposite the maharanee, like an ordinary woman on an outing of which she is uncertain, and I stretched out my long arm from which the henna flowers were already fading quickly. The teacup and saucer sat in my hand, light as a lily. I think the teaset may have been Meissen because Meissen comes in that shade of deep Chinese yellow to match my tunic exactly that day, and it is not impossible someone had watched my arrival to gauge the colour of my clothes so teacups could please me by matching perfectly. Things are like that in India. They do things of that sort in India. There were many things about that afternoon that were more eloquent than words: china to match my clothes, the door in the wall opening magically for me before my hand could reach the catch, the rainbows reflected from the fountains that began to play the instant I entered the garden, the men with the carpets for me to walk upon every inch of the way to the sitting-room, and the sitting-room itself, empty of anyone but two ladies having a cup of tea. I think I was made welcome, as much as was possible, and I think they wished me to be happy and to know they wished me no harm.

"Biscuit?" said the maharanee. "Or would you rather have a piece of cake." There was a chocolate cake on a stand, square and forbidding, the icing whitening faintly at the edges. It looked, as I recall, slightly stale, but they might have had it sent especially all the way from Delhi. That was one of the customs as well. She handed me a little plate and a fork for the cake and a napkin embroidered with yellow silk thread. Above our heads there was a sudden flurry as a pigeon flew in through the open doors to the balcony and it perched on the chandelier of dark green crystal far above our heads. I have never seen chandeliers made of green crystal anywhere else except in India, but this could be ignorance. I went from Hillingdon, where chandeliers of any sort do not abound, to India, so my experience with chandeliers in any colour was limited. The green chandelier glimmered above us in the shadows of the vaulted roof, and the pigeon sat amongst the prisms on one branch of it and stared down with bright small eyes as if it might be a spy sent there to listen and see.

I sit in my mother's kitchen writing this and I wonder who you are. Who are you, the person who reads this? The house has been bereft of light for so long that I leave what remains of the old blinds rolled high in the window frames. I love the moonlight and the light of day. The mice and rats have chewed the fringes of the blinds so they hang in rags like the remnants of dreams and they flutter in the draught from warped and shrunken casements. When the moon is high in the sky, and full as a big golden cheese, I can almost hear the house give a gasp at the illumination. Tonight, as I write this, it is very dark, the mean moon like a toenail paring above the old walnut tree. The rain is rumbling on the roof and it trickles down the old windows like tears.

Outside, the clothesline bears a burden of rampant honeysuckle, and the canopy of soft leaves and tendrils and sweet flowers turns the old frame and wires into a gazebo where hedgehogs rustle and spiders weave nests for eggs that look as big as peas. My own reflection in the dark windows is ephemeral but profound as I sit bent over the table, scribbling with an old pencil on sheets of yellowed paper. Nearly transparent, I am outlined against the flowers of the honeysuckle like a fallacy of vision glimpsed through a magic lantern. In this glassy image I have honeysuckle floating around my head, my mouth is ripe with rosehips from the old climber that has taken over any space left in the yard and my shoulders are garlanded with tendrils of green leaves. The two images — myself writing in the kitchen superimposed on the garden outside — become entangled in the reflection so it is difficult to know what is truth and what is fiction mirrored in the old glass tonight.

Night was falling when I returned to my pink stone house from the palace, the only time I ever went there. Gulab Kothari dropped me at my gates and drove away without speaking. I carried a small blue leather case I had not taken to the palace, but he made no remark about this and I did not explain it. I sat in the back of the car with the box on my knees and when he looked at me, as he often did, in the rear vision mirror I just gazed back at him as a tired woman does when she cannot be bothered to move.

"What did you talk about?" Netta wanted to know when I went inside. "What did she say? What did you do? What happened?"

What I never said to the maharanee, what she did not utter, were all more eloquent than anything we said. I never said, "Your husband never married me though he could have, he could have had two wives." She never said, "You stole Ranji away. You beguiled him with books and laughter." We did not say any of that.

"We talked about pigeon shit, on the chandeliers," I said to Netta.

"And after that?"

"Then we talked about monkey shit," I said, "on the chandeliers."

"And what happened then?"

"Then she showed me an aerosol one of her schoolfriends had sent from England, an aerosol cleaner for chandeliers, and I held the ladder while she climbed up and sprayed the prisms."

"I do not believe you, that she had a ladder. Why would she have a ladder in a palace, full of servants to do anything she wanted."

"It was a library ladder propped up against the bookcases. And she sprays the chandeliers herself, in secret, because no one else will do it properly. I helped her. I held the ladder while she sprayed the chandelier."

"What did she say then?"

"She said it was very nice to have someone to help her, to hold the ladder. She said it was nice."

"And what did you do then?"

"Then we had a piece of cake and she gave me a present."

"Ah," said Netta and I could tell this had pleased her. "A present."

I am very tall. I felt crass and large in that exquisite little drawing-room where the crystal side tables and the tea table were made by Lalique and monkeys and pigeons defaecated on the light fittings, an odd contradiction and one that is very Indian. Look beneath the surface of a beautiful sight and you have a corpse in a river, drifting like sticks in the light of day and removed by evening when the moon comes up because Captain Kothari has gone to the gate house and asked for it to be taken away. Even the method of taking the body away would have been very Eastern, very blurred, because it would have been taken away without being taken away, truth and falsehood laced to form a myth. There were screens up on the marble steps that overlooked the river as the moon rose, but I looked behind them and there was no body below. Someone had perhaps waded out and re-tethered it just round a bend, behind a rock, had placed it out of sight so it became both truth and fiction. Gone but not gone. I remember seeing a small bush that I did not recall from the afternoon. Someone might have crowned the body with a felled thorn tree. So the twigs and branches of the body might have still drifted in the same current, cloaked by the twigs and branches of a bush.

I felt tall and ungainly sitting on the maharanee's blue sofa, and I refused to curl myself up to make myself seem smaller. She was very tiny and I knew that she, also, had come from the south. She had been a princess from one of the southern states and her exquisite mother had remained beautiful till the day she died. That was more gossip from the markets, probably true. I also came from the south but my south was a different south. My south was Hillingdon. The maharanee wore a sari of turquoise silk, and through the draperies over her head I saw long earrings of onyx and diamonds hanging to her shoulders, brushing a heavy necklace of yellowing squarecut stones like a yoke that glimmered only faintly through the chiffon. Old diamonds have a hidden watery glitter that is like a riddle of light on a river at night, where a body floats under a bush and so is said to be gone.

"If you'd just steady it a bit," said the maharanee, her voice as soft as a sigh, "it won't take a moment." The can of aerosol cleaner was like a little baton in her tiny hand. I felt gross, enormous, leaning against the ladder, my hands looking suddenly square and capable, with a slight dusting of freckles. Her shoes were made of black satin, sewn with onyx beads around the toes, and the soles were hardly worn. I looked up at the twin fullstops of the maharanee's tiny heels above my head and they looked about the size of a bullet in the brain to put you out of your misery. To put me out of my misery.

"Coming down now," she said. "If you'd just hold this?" She handed me the can. "There." She had come down the rungs now, standing on the bottom one to regard the chandelier.

"Do you think that will be all right?" Each of her words was clearcut as one of the stones round her neck, and we stood there like conspirators, or like sisters helping each other. I have little recollection of family life, of any warmth from my sister. We were very different. Perhaps — and I wondered this as I helped the maharanee — we were merely dissimilar, not disaffected. Perhaps this is another facet of my life about which I was comprehensively wrong.

"I'm not sure," I said. "I have little experience in such things. Did your friend say it was good?" Do sisters talk like this? I stood there, wondering.

"Oh, excellent. Excellent." She sounded like a small jolly girl at school again. "Sybil said it was just the thing for the job."

"Then it will be, won't it?" I was encouraging, like a hopeful advertiser. It's funny how you can listen to yourself. For years I had wondered if I might ever go to the palace. I wondered if I would be invited to one of the big receptions for foreign guests, where perhaps I could be filtered into the group without comment or explanation, jewelled and clad in my own finery, looking like an intriguing woman of quality. And I would talk of Chaucer and Cicero, quoting poetry and sayings from literature, even singing a snatch of a song or two from Shakespeare. I would be an erudite charmer of specialised loveliness. But, when I did eventually go there, I just stood holding the old ladder in my yellow muslin tunic and little earrings like any ordinary woman could buy in an Indian market and I said, "What happens to the shit now?" It was a form of defiance, I think. Like the language of clothing which can be eloquent and subversive, the language of actual words can contain many meanings beyond the literal interpretation of what is uttered. What I really said was that I was a free person and would be leaving soon because I had adjudged it time to do this. It was my time to go and I would do so. No need to worry about me or fret about my motives because there were none. I could do as I pleased, and would. I could behave as well, or as badly, as I chose.

"Ah," she said. I think she was laughing. "What happens to the shit now is that it is foamed away like magic and any little pieces that fall are turned to bubbles and will be gathered up from the carpets in the morning by the Electrolux."

She saw me glance out the open doors, to the balcony above the courtyard. The sun was slanting in there now because it was late afternoon, nearly evening, and the sacred monkeys were playing on the columns, hanging from each other's tails and screaming about fights in the night.

"But we will not be here then, you and I," she said. "We will both be gone, and before you go I wish to give you something. I have this for you," she said, "and I wish you to take it." And that was when she handed me one of two blue leather boxes standing on the crystal table, predictably beside the chocolate cake but of more lasting worth and intrinsic merit.

"Go on," she said. "Open it." So I lifted the lid.

"Put it on," she said, so I held out my hands with the freckles and they suddenly looked much smaller, daintier and pristine as if she had made me lovely with her kindness. I took the diadem from the box and put it on my head. The stones matched the blaze of blue from the rug under her desk and the silk sashes across the breasts of the princes in the portraits. When I looked at her she had taken another the same from the other box and so we crowned ourselves, for want of anything better to do, on that eerie day when the only sound was the shrieking of the sacred monkeys and the sound of water from the fountains down in the garden.

"I don't believe you, that you held a ladder while she sprayed the chandelier for pigeon shit," said Netta when I arrived home. "And what was this present that the maharanee gives you," she said. So I showed her what was in the box.

"She likes you. I have always said this, that she likes you." There was a long silence.

"What was the ladder like, madam?" said Netta. "The ladder that you held for her while she sprayed the chandelier for pigeon shit and then she climbed down and you ate chocolate cake and she gave you a crown? What was this ladder like, madam?" So I knew then that Netta believed me, about what had happened. The language of language goes far beyond the meaning of the words used. Netta believed me and this story about how I went, at last, to the palace and the maharanee and I crowned ourselves with sapphires set in matching diadems of platinum and white gold while we ate a piece of chocolate cake and the monkeys screamed and fought while they pulled each others' tails.

It is evening now. Wallace and I have walked down to the boundary of The Arsehole's place and it is quiet down there. His house sits amongst the trees in a brooding silence, curtained windows shut like eyes masked by lids to hide the mood within. A car I have never seen before is parked in front of The Arsehole's house, a car painted a lurid shade of peacock blue, almost luminous. It is a colour that is without subtlety, like a rude joke that is not funny, a crass remark that is unnecessary. I presume, perhaps wrongly, that the father-in-law and/or the brother have arrived.

Wallace and I wade through the long grass to my garden shed because the door is now ajar and up till now it has been closed and fastened with a chain and padlock. The chain is hanging in pieces, the padlock is lying on the floor, and the shed door stands open. Within is a scene of disorder, but the disorder is different from usual. Certainly the old garden overalls still hang from the rafters like a person crucified, but their attitude is altered now. Someone has pulled them this way and that and a pocket is now torn off so the mythical crucifixion has now been accompanied by tormentings. Hands have pushed wheelbarrows to the bottom of the pile, some paint is overturned and a stream of an ancient thick cream colour winds through the dust on the floor. An unknown person has cut some rope with the garden clippers. It is more disordered than when last I looked in here, and the disorder is newly accomplished by hands that are unkind. The Arsehole and his cohorts have obviously had an inspection of what they plan to claim, and when I go back to the old wire fence with its lacings of bindweed and kikuyu grass there is a solidity about the silence from the house below mine, an intensity about the darkness from within that makes me imagine, again perhaps wrongly, that it is peopled with uncharitable secret watchers. Even silence has its own language if you study it carefully.

The ebullient and inestimable Goldblatt is still away in Sydney cavorting with Gloria Thorpy and there is no hope yet of any relief from worry about my boundaries and the shed and even my father's rusting old lawnmowers.

"Hup, hup." I am tapping Wallace on the left knee. "Hup, hup." And he is rearing up on his hind legs, myself a diminutive figure beside him but valiant, stick in hand. He trumpets twice, a blast that shatters the calm of the valley, and we return to the house, wading up through the long grass on the ramps that lead to the top garden, traversing the old seaward lawn that once my father mowed with the Morrison reel mower so it would make stripes like you see on cricket pitches. You would wonder why The Arsehole, or anybody, would plot to claim a rusty garden shed full of obsolete equipment once used with pride by a man who is dead, but I think the pleasure of the chase is what emboldens him, the lust for blood of the innocent, the obscure pleasure of causing terror and pain to strangers who mean no harm.

Twilight brings a silvery calm to the garden and on the way back to the house we find a line of red knitting wool winding through the trees on my side of the boundary. The Arsehole, or someone from his house, has tied the wool to a tree down the bottom of the garden and has taken it on a wide arc to a camellia at the top, the shape of the curve more or less like that of a banana and taking in a large area of my mother's former garden, now wilderness. But it is mine, wilderness or not.

Wallace, without instructions, pulls the wool with his trunk and it breaks, pinging away into the trees like elastic. The silence and darkness from The Arsehole's house is still profound but the instant we are round the back of my mother's house lights must have flashed on, activity must have begun, because I see the place jewelled with bright windows when I look out from the pantry. It has upset Wallace, the excursion to the lower garden, the smell of strangers in the shrubbery, the wool flicking away amongst the lawsonianas of my wind-break on the southern boundary. Perhaps even the ominous silence and darkness of The Arsehole's house caused Wallace a disquiet that makes him restless, so he trumpets wildly now, the note cracked and almost hysterical. So it is time for another reading because nothing quietens him as much as my voice, which could be like that of a mother with a frightened child, the sound rising in the wind, my reassuring silhouette against the moon, the flutter of my chiffon tunic in the evening breeze. If Wallace ever had a mother he has forgotten her long ago and he looks at me with a singular supplication, hugely humble and gentle beside the bird bath from which he often drinks.

But tonight I wear the diadem the maharanee gave me because it is a ridiculous and terrifying situation I am in here, and I might as well answer the powerful terrors of others with some of my own displays of power, even if they are laughable and ineffectual. So crowned like a little Neptune with a circlet of precious stones more blue than the sea, and sceptred with the handle of the old garden rake in my hand, I sit and read to Wallace about my old journey to India. The wind rises as darkness filters over the garden — Hillingdon is a windy place — and it puffs out my draperies so I seem bigger, an illusion of size like the swelling of a fighting bird when it fluffs out its feathers. It is going to be a battle about the garden shed, but as I read I become gentle and beautiful again. The words take hold and make me their courteous servant, a warden of language. I am a sincere liegeman of the beauty of words as night falls on the city and the moon rises to shine in my window on the mysteries of Captain Kothari's letter. *Yours very, very sincerely. With kindest admiration and regards.*

"Why is the house in darkness? Why hasn't she got the lights on? What does she think she's playing at?" My father might have said that, something like it anyway, when the taxi dropped them at the gates after bridge. "Heigh ho, there aren't any lights on." It was one of his conversational mannerisms to say, "Heigh ho."

They would have tramped up the drive towards their own unlit house, over my skid marks on the gravel, through the gates left swinging open in a rising wind, as far as the open doors of the car shed and then they would have seen the Cortina was gone. The eau-de-Nil treasure, polished every Sunday, was absent. Subsequently, they would have discovered I was gone as well. The order of these discoveries is significant.

No light would have been shining at any window. The dishes from dinner were left stacked beside the sink to drip dry. I am not untidy but my tidiness is always reasonable, only that which it is possible to attain without a fuss within the framework of circumstances prevailing at the time. Add pedantry to my crimes. On an ordinary night I would have dried the dishes and put them away in the tall cupboard that housed the crockery. It was not an ordinary night, though, and I had had other things to do. Choosing what book to take with me. Putting it in the bag. Selecting the chintz opera coat. Opening the safe. Deciding how much money I might need for petrol and contingencies. Taking the money. It took a while. Putting some money back in the safe. I took only what was absolutely necessary, skinned down to the very bone. And I was still called a thief. Goldblatt, in his first annual letter, refers to me as a thief.

The boughs of the old trees that lined the drive spilled out wildly beyond the reach of my father's ladder and his cruel annual pruning saw. Branches must have thrashed over the heads of my parents as they approached the house on the dark thread of the front path, thence to their dark house and the dark news that the place was daughter-less as well as car-less. I do not know how long it would have been till they discovered that my mother's chintz coat was missing from the downstairs cloakroom under the stairs or that I had got into my father's safe and taken a small amount of money. I left a lot behind and this is not to my credit. If life were just a

106

rehearsal for what we do officially later, then the next time I left I would have taken everything in the safe and would have deserved the title 'thief'. It was given to me, anyway. I should have ensured that I earned it.

I turned away from that house and everything in it, and I went southward after I skidded in gravel beside the gate posts. Underneath my father's trees violets were beginning to flower, a short-stemmed variety that was unpickable and I knew they lay like secrets beneath the clipped grass. I could smell their lingering scent in the car for miles down the road, so you could say I left the house to travel through the eye of a hurricane but that the wind brought with it, for me, the benediction of the essence of violets as a charm for my journey. The holy man who has come from Agra would say that this was a very auspicious sign. Some of the winter-blooming trees, like camellias and rhododendrons, were showing faint swellings of buds that would have a hint of colour in a month. Later the roses would be pruned. But I drove away through the moonlit landscape, and first of all I went southward leaving everything behind, everything I had looked after so carefully for the past year.

The wind was springing up even then. If I had listened to the radio, if I had heard the weather forecasts predicting the hurricane, I think I still would have set off on my journey and perhaps I would then have travelled with greater fear because I would have known what I was doing. I proceeded, though, in a state of innocence and mystery, blindly driving into the heart of the storm, always believing that the fault lay in my own ineptitude when the car almost veered into drains, would not take bends. As I went I saw the branches of other people's trees tossing against the lit windows of unknown houses and the light now seemed to flicker through the trees as though the dwellings might be on fire, as if what I really saw was not just illumination but the beginning of conflagrations engulfing all homes. I drove south, under a moon so bright it seemed hysterical, and the car skidded again in loose gravel at the crossroads on the edge of town where the lights ceased and the dark hills awaited. Until then I had somehow believed I was flying through the night, but my own rashness made me afraid so I took the southern fork in the road in a sober frame of mind, suddenly old and careful as a retired nurse gone to seed. I might have been going to visit an elderly relative on an unhappy outing, perhaps to bandage an

ulcerated foot or leg in a house that smelt of cats. I drove as carefully as that.

Before I left I had spread out all the road maps on the floor of the
upstairs hall and I traced with one thin finger the route I must take
through all those small towns. When that southward road wound
down and down forever, down a great hill beyond one of them —
and already I had forgotten its name — I must turn left, I must go
eastward then to link up with a road to the north. I had to travel
many miles, for nearly three hours, before I could finally take that
road I sought to the north. You would wonder why I had to take
such a circuitous route, such a wayward journey round three sides
of a square, to finally get where I was going, but it was the manner
in which the land was disposed, you see. It was the geography.
There was no passage straight through the mountains and the
forests between where I lived and the seaport I was aiming for. I
could show you easily enough on the map and you would see what
I mean immediately. There was no other way to it, no quicker way,
than the road I took south, then east and north.

As I swung south at the crossroads I added up all the timings
again and it always came out as an uncomfortable and untenable
answer, a dangerous proposition in the darkness. Drive southward for two hours through all the little towns lying low in the
moonlight, nothing to do there on a weekday night — and this was
a Tuesday — except eat your dinner, read the Lost and Founds in
the local rag and go to bed. Lost: One daughter, librarian, quiet,
golden hair, now aged 27. Found: One maharaja, fond of reading,
honours degree in literature, Caius College, Cambridge, aged 49.
Turn eastward a short way south of a little town where the main
road winds down and down forever to the base of a range of wild
hills. Another good and meaty hour of driving till the north road
descends slowly, mean as a grudge, from more dark hills. At least
three hours so far, and more to come. Perhaps two hours of travelling north to the port after that, depending on the weather and the
road conditions. Just a plain there, miles and miles of plain, just
flat driving after a gorge at the beginning of the northern road.
Simple, I thought. Once I hit the northern road I'm nearly there,
a whisper away.

I knew nothing of the storm then, nothing about the hurricane
that tore the land apart as I travelled through it, sometimes abreast

of me, and occasionally I drew ahead so I was the precursor of destruction in some places.

Forwards/backwards, backwards/forwards; no matter how I added it up the arithmetic always came out the same. Two hours south, a good hour east, two hours north equals five hours in all. It was exactly seven o'clock when I left my father's dark house with its reproachful unlit windows, the garage doors swinging in a flurry of the wind. So I would get to the ship about midnight. It awaited my arrival. Registered in Monrovia, with a name that altered according to destination or cargo and a Hindu crew that seldom altered because they had nowhere else to go and nothing awaiting them when they got there if they ever did, it was waiting for me and perhaps I was in much the same state as that crew, only I was slightly better dressed and had more hope for the future. An entire ship, and its full complement of crew, waited for me. At the beginning of my peculiar and specialised journey across the world to become, inaccurately, a fair-haired and wheaten-skinned changeling reputed, again inaccurately, to have come from the north, a rusty little ship tarried and dawdled, rocking at anchor as the sea rose before the cyclone.

I took the car south on that deserted road and seven o'clock became eight and then nearly nine, and still I did not find the turning that would lead me eastwards to the third leg of my journey, the northern road. That wanton golden moon sulked behind the clouds now, and one small town after another lay behind me, but I did not find the road that would take me east. The wind was very strong and I thought a storm must be brewing further north. I think now that it was better not to know the truth of the matter — that I travelled within the framework of that cyclone like its broken heart and I sometimes cried from fear that I would never find the east road. I would have wept from a much greater terror if I had known, truly, what I did and where I was. It was better not to know.

The holy man from Agra says a thousand reasons for worry and anxiety, day after day, oppress the fool but not the wise man. But I think, that night, I proceeded southwards unworried in a greater sense, though disquietened in a small way about the eastern road, because I was a fool. It was the exact opposite of what the holy man says. If I had been wise I would have listened to the weather forecasts and stayed at home. If I had been wise I would have stayed at home anyway because what more foolish journey could there be on such a night than to go across your own country in the darkness, driving hundreds of miles around three sides of a geographical square of mountains and impenetrable forests to meet a man you hardly know from a land you have never seen and, later, to begin to travel there on an unknown and mysterious ship sailing under whatever flag may be expedient at the time. Yet, like a mathematician using the wrong formula for the right logarithm, my answer was correct in the end. I did arrive. Like a final answer, with all numbers in the proper order and in the right margins, I did get there. A little crumpled, perhaps. Grubby. Tired. Dirty, even. I might have been filthy. The mushroom-coloured chintz opera coat was never the same again, but did it need to be? I was never the same again, and definitely I did not need to be so. It was an excellent and wonderful journey, made better by its infinite terribleness.

From where I am sitting now I can see monkeys bounding along my walls and ramparts and an old man sits, cross-legged, on the path outside my house, tipping water over himself from a tin bowl. There are no children today playing and laughing amongst my flowers but perhaps some will come tomorrow. Netta can always put the sweetmeats and the good plain food away for another day. I love to hear children playing in my garden. The desert is beginning — my house is on the very outskirts of the city — and against the grey of the wastelands the open pink mouths of the monkeys look alarmingly rosy, the teeth too white and sharp as they snarl in fights over territory. The dusty ground is greyish yellow with a scattering of rocks. There are patches of rough weeds but much of the land is bare. Old Persian roses bloom within the confines of my garden, though, because there are fountains here. I have water, as much water as I can use and plenty left over. Water is wealth here.

People here revere the monkeys and they feed them, but they hate the monkeys on their roofs. Sometimes a troup of monkeys will take up residence on a particular roof, using it as a base for their forays. Monkeys are noisy. Monkeys shit and dribble. But I love the monkeys because they are effervescent. Monkeys do what people wish they had the courage to accomplish, but do not. What man, occasionally, would not wish to march up to another and bite him till the blood runs because he has proved himself an enemy? What mother would not wish to hold her child against her body forever like the monkeys do? It seems like forever as I watch from my balcony, but it is probably only for a season, which is forever for the monkeys. I share the water here with the monkeys, and I leave the gates to my garden open so people, like the old man outside right now, can find my pools and fountains. People can fill their bowls and beakers. They can bathe. They can pick my roses for their feast days, and they can bring their children here to eat and play. The journey here, through the cyclone, was worth it because it changed me from an unwanted librarian, originator of a slop on the pavement, to a generous seraph.

The night I drove my father's car to meet the ship I could not find that eastern road. Sometimes the moon came out suddenly from behind the clouds, like a surprise from better times, and it lit my way along the ridges of the hill country. I was convinced then that I was not lost. When the clouds scudded over it again I became equally certain that I had somehow missed the turning, that I would be a truant forever in a foreign landscape where morning would not come. I had not recognised the little towns I passed through. The night was so dark I missed the signs that stated their names. Sometimes I thought I kept driving through the same settlements, always in circles and back again to the same broken fence, to oddly similar five-barred gates.

My father was not a man who liked picnics. Picnics conjure up an idea of unexpectedness, of tiny accidents of fate turned to delight like when a driver might stop to consult a map and suddenly see a fine view, glimpse a mossy rock beside a river. We were not a family who picnicked. We did not go on country drives or stop without prior plan to have an ice-cream at a country store. We did not suddenly stop on country roads to explore secondhand shops in old dairy factories, to answer signs on the side of the road that said 'Cut Flowers For Sale. Apply Within.'

My father went places on business, with the appointments set beforehand, if he had clients to see, promises to keep. I remember once, when I was a child, noting his bewilderment when I set off down the road on my bicycle.

"Where are you going?" he said. He was a punctilious father, but without spontaneity.

"I don't know," I said.

"Well, why are you going, Margaret?"

111

"To see what it's like," I said.

"And where are you going to stop."

"I'll know where to stop when I see something interesting." I rode away. I remember his bewilderment, the puzzlement in his eyes, as he watched me go. I don't think he could understand uncertainty, adventure if you like. He liked a recipe for everything, a formula. I don't think he lived. I think he proceeded through the evolvement of a human being at all stages from birth to death, according to plan.

"That child is a real problem," I heard him say to my mother the day I rode away on my bicycle on an uncharted miniature expedition to see things I did not know for certain were actually there.

The moon came out again as I drove down a winding road through a series of deep valleys and I was convinced by then that I had passed the road I sought, that I was lost. I cried. I wept with reticence and composure — I was not my father's daughter for nothing — so the tears just rolled down my cheeks and dripped on to the front of my mother's coat. I'll tell you a way you can judge your own age. You can tell, irrevocably, if you are growing old, and one can be old at any age, if you cry without paroxysms and weep without feeling so the tears just roll down your cheeks. Then you are old and have given up hope. I should have had more faith in myself. I should have remembered to read the concentric circles on the map that showed height above sea level and I would have known as I drove down into the last shallow valley that I was approaching my eastern road. I should have remembered that the circles lay on the map like the mark of a tide upon sand and at their exact centre I would find my road.

It lay beneath yellow sulphurous lights, marked with large signs and arrows, and again it struck me that everything was so empty that night, as if the world cleared itself away for my passage. I had never seen the main road so devoid of traffic, the intersections almost ghostly with lack of cars. I turned into the dark eastern road which was narrower, just a strand between hills and then there was not even a sign of a light anywhere. No hillside showed a glint of a farmer's dwelling. The story I have since read in The Times says that electricity failed over a wide area. There is usually a simple explanation.

It is useless to speculate on the meaning of love. What is love to one person is not love to another. It was my idea of what love should

112

be like that set me off on my journey through those black hills the night of the storm when damage to property and to the land itself was a legend by late the following day. By that time, though, I was at sea and it is to my infinite discredit that I was probably darning the captain's socks. I told him I couldn't sit about doing nothing till we docked in Sydney and I could catch my plane, so he gave me his socks to darn. The holes were not large and the socks were silk and so was the matching thread he gave me. But, still, I would have been darning socks.

"I'm lost," I said to a man at a petrol station. I had come upon a little gathering of houses, all in darkness, with a general store and a petrol station, a sudden surprise in the gloom of that night. The petrol gauge in the car was showing 'Low'. The journey had been longer than I had expected. I swooped in, under the canopy, so suddenly I think I gave the man a fright. He was counting change in the office and I had to toot the horn twice before he came out. The wind was very fierce then. I was afraid to open the car door in case it blew away. I watched him coming out towards me, doubled up in the wind.

"You've picked a fine night," he said. His eyes were a cold blue and he seemed bad-tempered, but he may have been tired or even frightened. It was a frightening night.

He told me there was a hurricane.

"Are you sure?" I said. I heard my own voice, quite cold and measured.

"Of course I'm sure," he said. "Where've you been, lady — asleep?" He was the sort of man who calls everyone 'lady' if he doesn't like them. That sort of man. "Been away with the dicky birds or something?"

"Will you fill the car up with petrol," I said. It might have been a fine clear evening in the middle of a nice and pretty city and myself, well-dressed, going off to dinner somewhere suitable. I have always preferred unsuitable places. "Please." I did not make it a question. It was a little statement, like a bullet.

The night was dark and cold, though, and he was running the place on an emergency generator. He might have been alarmed. He told me all about the storm, about the radio broadcasts telling everyone to stay at home. He almost threw the hose into the petrol tank of my father's Cortina and I think he might have chipped the paint

113

but I never bothered to check later. It was too late in every possible way.

"You been asleep or something?' he said. "Coming out on a night like this. Where are you going, for God's sake?"

I told him, and I said, "I didn't think it would be so far." And that is another instance of my quaint ideas clashing with reality. I thought, and when I thought it I knew it was wrong, that because I wanted the journey to the ship to be calm and clear and short it would be. Untrue. My whole difficulty with life is that I think of it as a literary exercise with agendas written to suit my dreams, the alignments all perfect like dove-tailed joints made by a better cabinetmaker. If I were writing the journey I would have made it short.

"You must be mad," he said.

"Yes." I spoke without any rancour because I believed it. I believed I must be mad, in a nice kind of way. Not dangerous. You know the sort of thing. Just quirky, and batty, but lovely.

My father, only two days before, had taken us to a cricket match. "But I don't like cricket," I said then. "I don't know how you play it."

"Margaret," my father said, "will you, please, just do something that your mother and I want, without a fuss? You give me the very definite impression that you've just about driven yourself mad. Please, do not drive your mother and me mad as well. Will you, please, just do as I ask, just for once? It's quite a curiosity, this match. There's a lot of local interest, the Indian team's travelling with a maharaja as the manager, and your mother's set her heart on having afternoon tea in the tea tent and meeting him. I think she wants to wear that new pink hat. She's set on the idea of going as a family, having a family day out. Please just do something without a fuss for once."

I don't know what I expected. I stayed by the entrance to the tent because it was hot inside and I don't usually eat afternoon tea. My mother and father seemed happy, talking to their friends. My father was on some committee or another. He had a badge to wear, and my mother had her new pink hat — another sort of badge. I stood, leaning against one of the tent poles and I said, to nobody, "'Whose woods these are I think I know.'" Robert Frost. One of my favourite poets. The cricket ground is quite wooded round the edges. There are lines of large old trees, little hollows with miniature forests where the people sit in the shade to watch matches.

I heard another voice reply, "'His house is in the village, though.'" The next line in the poem, so someone else knew Frost. I looked around and there, leaning against another tent pole, was this smallish man, rather tanned, with a thin face. He had very dark, thoughtful eyes. He asked what I was doing there and I said, "My father made me come to meet some bloody maharaja, but I won't," I said. "I can't be bothered."

"Well, don't," he said. "Don't bother. Stay here with me and talk to me about Robert Frost. I'd like that." My father must have regretted the whole day, beginning with my mother's pink hat, which didn't suit her and the flower on the side fell off before the third over.

The night I drove to meet the ship that man at the service station pleased me. He made me laugh because he made me feel like a ruffian flying through the darkness, a vagabond disguised as a dirty traveller. By then my tears had dripped all down the front of the coat.

"You're the first car I've seen for three hours," the man said. "And if you've come from the west, from the north-west, you've got through the worst of it." Perhaps he was trying to be encouraging. Not far away from there I found my northern turning, just as he said I would.

"Not far," he shouted after me as I drove away. "Not far."

I laughed then, in my dirty coat within the confines of a car that was now filthy. I must have come through mud somewhere because the car was grimed with it past the windows.

As for my ideas of what love is? I equate it with being lost, to travel without knowing one's destination, to be blinded by the wind and mud and yet drenched in the scent of old violets from a garden many miles away. To see a stranger leaning on a tent pole and to know irrevocably that one would look at no one else. When we had been talking about Robert Frost for a long time I went closer to him, this small man with the thin face, and I put my hand on his shoulder. "Please," I said, "will you tell me who you are?"

The moon went behind the clouds again when I took the northern road. There was now no hint of light, no sign of brightness anywhere as I drove north through that lost landscape. I sensed that great hills reared up beside the road and once or twice, above the noise of the wind, I heard the sound of water, a small and regular babble like that from a small stream. I imagined a nice little river, a pretty little rill running sweetly over stones. It was an elegant thought to savour as I wound my way through the high country, but the reality was probably that the sound came from a drain swollen by floodwater and filled with mud.

Later I heard water again, but this time the sound was the swirling of a torrent and I thought there must have been a flood. The road in that part was very wet and deeply veined with runnels and potholes. When the car lurched into these, brown water splashed up over the windscreen to blind me for a moment. I became frightened then, without the moon to guide me, and drove north very slowly. Later, when the moon came out again with renewed brilliance, bright and bold, I looked in the rear vision mirror and saw a range of vile dark hills with granite escarpments that fell to the beds of swamps but I had already, blinded by darkness, come through all that. So I sang as I drove then, and the big bold moon lit the way for me while the countryside seemed to open out into a broader and more generous landscape without the sudden tantrums of torrents or cliffs. Fooled again.

Not far from that the road fell into a great gorge, deeply flooded and veined with slips of rock and earth. I edged past bulldozers and road machinery and flashing red lights that lined the single lane. There was one car ahead of me. At first I could not believe I had seen its lights but I drove closer, so close I could see the bare shoulders of the driver in my own car lights, and they were deeply tattooed in swirls and waves like a map of the ocean's lost floor. 'Don't Panic' was painted across the rear window and I was soothed and charmed by this message. The holy man from Agra would say that it was sent to me by design from positive forces and this may be true, or not. You might say the tattooed driver in the car with the painted message was as mad as I was to be out on such a night and that he was probably going to collect his drycleaning or visit a sick uncle. The message heartened me, though, so in tandem we made our way slowly through that devilish part of the countryside unlit by the stars and with only the fitful glimmer of a moon mostly obscured by clouds. Only the winking red lights guided us along what remained of the road and I could tell, by the sound the tyres made, that sometimes we drove over planks spanning chasms for the noise was hollow and reverberating like the strains of distant rage.

I constantly read the little sign that said 'Don't Panic' and was thus reassured that perhaps the other driver, in strange guise, was an imp or angel sent to guide me through the night. You can see from this that not only do I possess the great fault of being too literary, I am also too nice and too pretty in some of my thoughts. Probably the tattooed man was a burglar going home, or going out to steal, or he may have been heading for the nearest pub to have a beer. When I wound down the window of my car I heard, as if from a remote land, music from his car stereo so he must have had the volume turned up very loud for me to do this over the sound of the wind and water. The cadences echoed over the drumming of the tyres and the sound of the weather, like the voices of gnomes or elves. So we passed through the last of the high lands and went down into those wide plains I had seen marked on the map. I had travelled towards them for so long, since after the sun set and the forgotten moon rose. It was by then, I knew, becoming very late.

Far away, on hillsides, I saw the lights of farmhouses again and, further ahead, was the glow of a city. There must have been better emergency generators in that part of the country, or perhaps the storm did not hit so hard when the gorge ended. I do not know. Much of what I write here in the holy man's ivory book is conjecture. It is only what I saw and thought and may contain falsehoods or misconstructions. But I believe it to be true. I drove steadfastly because I could see the city I had aimed for and even though it was still far away I knew I would arrive there now, that I was not lost. My calculations, in their wild and hopefully inaccurate way, had come out right like my own curious personal logarithm about my own life. Wrong numbers, wrong process, right answer; something like that, anyway.

I had lost my angel with his music. Whether he had disappeared when I no longer needed him — the holy man would say this was the answer — or whether he had taken to the dark hills again, sliding away from the main road down a track I had not noticed, I do not know. So now I drove slowly through the murky plains alone again except for an occasional rabbit mesmerised by my headlights or the sight of the slanting rain like rods of wire against fences black with mud and sleet.

That sweet straight road took me cleanly northward after I finally came down from the last of the hills, but I did not look at my watch. It was very late, I knew that much, and I preferred not to know the full extent of this. I had been told the ship could wait till midnight.

As I went I began to sing the only song I knew right through. 'Waltzing Matilda'. When you think of it, an oddly suitable choice for someone like I was that night. The collar of the pink chintz opera coat was still wrapped round my throat like the crushed wings of a butterfly, and I sang. The headlights picked out the rough painted line in the middle of the road as a marker as I drove. A detour took me away from the main road a few miles north of a railway crossing and I drove round a clay bluff on a dirt road, the car nearly floating in the mud. There was another line of those red lights left by a road gang, so I followed them, blinded and drifting in the darkness, and as I went along I counted them. When I reached a magical twenty-four I was back on the road again. I remember being happy when I was twenty-four. I think of it as a lucky number.

But the dark landscape and the glimmer of the distant houses of the city guided me gently away from the storm. When I passed through a small settlement, lit this time, I stopped at another petrol station.

"Could you tell me, please, if I'm lost?" I said to the man who came out from the office. He had peered out first, through the steamy windows of an inner room, but he came out into the night without any suspicion of harm. His face was perfectly serene. I suppose he saw a woman in a sort of grubby mushroom-coloured raincoat, tired, a woman with tired eyes, leaning against a very dirty car. What harm would I do anyone? I, catching his innocence, stood there as guileless as any girl on an errand.

"I'm frightened I might be lost," I said to him, "and yet I know I'm not."

"No, indeed," he said when I told him where I wanted to go, "you're spot on."

I bought some chocolate and while he fetched it from the counter I just stood there, dazed by the driving and the weather, looking out into the darkness from that brightly lit forecourt and I felt like a creature brought in from the cold.

"How much longer will it take me to get there?" I gave him some of my father's money, from the safe at home, for the chocolate. It was only a dollar and I was very hungry by then. They should not have called me a thief. If my daughter had lived I would have gladly given her anything of mine, and I did give her something. She had long thin fingers, beautiful fingers. They didn't know I saw her, on the pavement, just for a moment. She might have been a pianist. I have always been musical, so I gave her that — the gift of fading music, just for an instant.

"How much longer will it be, please," I said to the man at the petrol station. I told him where I had come from. "I've been travelling since before the moon rose."

"You mean since it was dark?" Another of my many crimes. To revere the charm and forget the gloom.

"Yes, since it was dark," I said, sensible and prosaic now. He was a very tall man and bent almost double to check the car's petrol cap was on securely even though I had bought no fuel there. I was glad of this care, I remember that. I felt like an errant daughter out too late at night and I suppose that is what I was. "Since exactly six fifty-nine." I can be as businesslike as anybody if I want to be.

"You've come a long way," he said, "and you've made good time." He glanced at his watch. "Another ten minutes, that's all. A scanty ten minutes, depending on how you go."

I reached the sea not long after that. The main road runs along beside the ocean for the last mile or two. I drove gently along then and the moon came out again to silver the highway in front of me. Upon this shining pathway I made my way quietly into the seaport, the car floating along with hardly a sound. I filtered over that last bit of countryside like a political plotter who imagines freedom is nearly at hand, or I might have been a mudlark on a jaunt, but always pure in heart. Pure in heart. The moon had swung through the sky, had catapulted itself in a great arc that looked far more than an evening's labour, so I did not look at my watch, did not wish to know the time because the idea of the hour frightened me. But the ship was there just as I had been told it would be. I left the car slewed across the Harbour Master's parking place and I walked along the wharf to the gangplank, which swung in the wind and rattled as I walked over it. The batons were far apart and through the gaps I could see the dark water with its frills of oily foam. Ahead the pilot launch was waiting to guide us out of the harbour.

"I would have waited another twenty minutes." The captain stepped out from the shadows. "Not any longer."

"Well, you didn't have to, did you, because I'm here already," I said. By then I was very cold and very hungry. Add rudeness to my other misdeeds. I didn't thank him for waiting because he had been told to wait. And paid heftily to wait. And I didn't thank him for taking me on board because that had been paid for as well. Perhaps that was the beginning of my becoming tough, of my becoming a peppery woman.

I was wearing an old rope of pearls around my neck. They were real but the colour and shape were uneven, and they were also secondhand. My mother had disliked and discarded them for those reasons. They were not a gift. I just took them over. I felt the weight of those warm pearls round my neck as I walked through the last of the wind. Pearls will warm to your flesh. And I had a battered silver bracelet on, too, set with sapphires so dark they were nearly black. Another of Mother's discards. Not new. Not bright. Too dented. I remember I sat on the little bunk in my cabin, which was very small and very plain, and I perched there swinging my legs like a girl on her first night at boarding school. In my bag I had a book, round my neck I had a string of pearls, a sapphire bracelet hung on my left wrist and I had some of my father's money still crushed into my wallet. That was all I had.

The ship's engines were turning over when I went on board and I heard them quicken, the sound of chains, perhaps the anchor chains. We seemed to be moving and I knew when we hit the open sea, beyond the harbour, because the ship began to bucket.

"Cocoa?" The captain had knocked at the door of the cabin. He held out a mug. It was a very simple ship, a rough ship. It was the sort of ship where they do not ask for your documentation, where a passport is not asked for. The sort of ship that figures on lists of suspicious things to be watched. I think the Indian crew mostly did for themselves, though the Indian cook produced the main meals and made nan every day, a sort of unleavened Indian bread that I have learned to like.

"Do you play chess?" he said. I felt it was some kind of concession. He might have thought he had been abrupt before.

"A bit." I play chess quite well, actually. I can play the concession game, too, if I wish. "If you had any sewing that needed doing I could do it for you," I said, "or anybody. If anybody had any darning I could do it." There was a long silence. "I don't like to sit about

120

twiddling my thumbs," I said. He looked at me as if I was not what he had expected and, considering my history and my forthcoming life, I can see I might not have been. He told me there were tickets awaiting me in Sydney, documentation being rushed through so I had the correct papers, a visa, a passport. I remember his eyes which were flecked with gold and they, in retrospect, remind me of the eyes of the holy man when he hands me the pen and says, "Sing to me, dreamer. Oh, sing to me, dreamer."

That was how I began my journey to India.

CHAPTER SEVEN

DIAMONDS AND PEARLS, pearls and gold, gold and turquoises. I am sorting through the contents of the plastic buckets full of jewellery, that wall of containers that bars the door to my old bedroom. At the bottom of the stairs, in the entrance hall, there is a clearing in the packed boxes of clothes and accessories and on an old linen sheet spread on the floor I sort through ropes of necklaces, handfuls of coins, tiny barbs from the catches of brooches pricking my fingers so everything is rubied with tiny drops of blood. The carrier is coming the day after tomorrow to collect all the packing, all the boxes labelled *Clothes from the 1940s, Charleston dresses of the 1920s,* and so on, all the items of furniture with labels tied to legs or knobs. *Walnut Grandfather Chair, Circa 1860. Matching Grandmother Chair, Ditto. Sheraton Revival Style Bedroom Suite, Four Pieces, in Burr Walnut. Walnut Loo Table. Set of Six Balloon-Back Chairs, Finely Carved.* There are walls of boxes, ramparts of crates, fences of bundles, and it is all to go off to an auction of antiques and vintage clothing catalogued and advertised nationally to attract collectors and dealers. The auction list down at the rooms will end with the cliché auction phrase "and many more items too numerous to mention". This describes my consignment perfectly. The carrier is sending a pantechnicon to collect it all, and may need to return for a second load. Unintentionally, over the passage of many years, my mother's magpie enthusiasm for shopping with and without discrimination has provided a bank of investments, a literal barricade of worth, a pile of money in every possible form, mostly disguised.

"What do you do all day by yourself in that ghastly old show," Goldblatt always asks me during our weekly appointments.

"Nothing." It is best to keep Mother's fortune a secret.

"Don't you get lonely? Doesn't time hang very heavily, Margaret?"

"No. I potter about at this and that." I am as vague as an idiot let out of somewhere for the day. No suspicion of what I am really doing must come into Goldblatt's mind. Fear and sudden insecurity have made me wily, suspicious and foxy. I do not like Goldblatt's constant nagging about signing things. His office safe, for valuables, seems very unsafe to me, and very unvaluable. I am vague, unspecific and deliberately dim.

"Sometimes I find a book and read it. Other times I might do a bit of sewing or something. I wouldn't worry about it, if I were you. I'm fine." The voice is as thin and misty as sleep before dawn.

Tonight it has become very late. I have been busy all day and far into the evening packing boxes and working round the house. The blue enamel and sterling silver clock tells me it is twenty past eleven. Midnight approaches. The yellow light from the hall lamp casts a mild glow over the scene of my sorting. None of the light bulbs in the house is above 40 watts so the illumination has a softness that makes the shadows behind the piles of boxes very deep, like thoughts that do not bear examination. Perhaps Mother liked to spend on clothes and jewellery what she saved in electricity. The influence of the house is such that I continue the parsimony out of quaint respect. During my forays to the supermarket down the road I have purchased smaller light bulbs, soap and disinfectant, scrubbing brushes and detergent, and the attention I have received has been deliberate and revealing. I have grown accustomed to the veiled glances and the deliberate stares, then the people look away as if it were a catching disease to wear turquoise chiffon tunics to the supermarket, it may be a specific illness to have a yoke of pearls about a neck. That soft and unspecific glow of my new, but modest, light bulbs makes me look almost pretty in the old hall mirror that is bloomed with dust. I look nearly like a young scholar with spectacles perched on the end of a pert nose and bent over a sweet and pretty task. I was like that once and now I resemble it again briefly in a grimy mirror, a myth of reflection because my spectacles are lost somewhere and my view of things is blurry round the edges.

There is a rampart of lidded plastic buckets across the door of my old bedroom and I let each one carefully down, through the stairwell, on the end of a piece of rope from the shed The Arsehole claims as his. We will fight over that little building, and everything it signifies, soon. In a place like Hillingdon where they are watching cricket on their televisions or listening to records of Bob Dylan in sitting-rooms spruce with William Morris upholstery, no one would imagine that a woman in an Indian tunic is sorting through buckets of jewellery and placing items in old shoe boxes labelled newly, in a fine and slightly foreign hand, *Diamonds, Cultured Pearls, Artificial Pearls, Sterling Silver, 18 Carat Gold, 9 Carat Gold*.

Wallace is outside, put to bed in the car shed, and silence on the property is impenetrable, the safety absolute because my activities are so bizarre, so improbable they might be beyond the imagination of any robbers. I hope so. And The Arsehole will be asleep by now. It is days till Saturday when I expect to take arms in the battle of the garden shed and Mother's half an acre of trees. The Arsehole will be resting, in preparation.

The brass heart I first saw when I was talking to Daphne on the telephone, a large lump of unlikely yellow, is 18 carat gold flecked with a sprinkling of pure gold dust, its chain stout enough to hold a bath plug, also violent yellow and similarly dusted. The magnifying glass shows me the markings, tells me so like a silent helper and friend. Myriad strings of coloured beads I imagined were glass are agate of various kinds. Their weight should have told me this when I stirred them with a foot after the first bucket spilt its contents on the floor of the pantry. This place is making me soft and slack, unvigilant, unknowledgeable. Real pearls feel gritty on the teeth, artificial pearls are slimy-smooth and valueless. I sit cross-legged in the hall, as midnight approaches, taking bites of pearls, juggling beads in my hands to feel the weight and the warmth, applying the magnifying glass to hallmarks. Agate and semi-precious beads are heavy. Artificial ones are sharp and light and cold. Things are weighed in my hands as if I am a usurer, a trader in a market. My stacks grow. The boxes of booty blossom through the entrance hall and up the stairs. *Rolled Gold. Rhinestone Brooches in the Cartier Style, 1920s. Agate Necklaces In Various Colours. Matching Earrings and Brooches. Cameos (Brooches, Rings, Etc). Sterling Silver Cigarette Cases and Compacts.* My packing grows as one o'clock comes and goes. As I take passing fancies to odd things I put them on and after an hour I am decked like a sultan's whore in a rainbow of colours and jewels, fingers blazing with the rings Goldblatt reported and also emeralds he never mentioned. Mother must have kept those a secret. Green was perhaps not her colour. She was very particular about accessorising things correctly — always navy with white, pink with blue, black with camel, red with cobalt. The emeralds may never have been worn. In a leather box that looks untouched there is a large emerald ring shaped like a leaf and set with twenty or thirty carats of small stones, like something a goblin king might wear in the depths of his forest, and a brooch in emeralds, peridots and beryls shading from green to palest yellow shows a dancer pirouetting forever on one vivid malachite jewelled toe. I keep these for myself. I would like to dance so happily always, and live in a forest like a goblin sprite. On a shoulder and upon one finger are placed my dreams, the golden jewel heart around my neck. There is no piece of jewellery showing a hand, though, and if there were I would claim that as well because it would be like my own hand-print upon a suttee gate, my palms dipped in red dye to leave my mark before I go out on a last journey to the fire. Living here is like being burnt but left alive; loneliness, fear and memory seer me. My suttee is cold and seems endless.

As I go upstairs for more loads to let down on the rope I begin to jingle, there is a faint sound of expensive metals and stones, the attrition of gold upon pearls, bracelet upon amulet, my ears on fire with ruby clusters and a matching ring on the little finger of my left hand. Mother did well in her sad and prodigal greed for possessions.

Sovereigns, Half Sovereigns, Assorted Krugerrands. By two o'clock in the morning I have a shoebox well filled with these. Nine carat gold-bar brooches set with three sovereigns, nine carat gold-bar brooches set with one sovereign, half sovereigns set as rings, half sovereigns set as pins, brooches clustered with small and large diamonds, brooches set with garnets and amethysts, pins trimmed with white and blue sapphires, more gold bar brooches set with pearls; I pack all these. When I lie down, fully clothed, on my truckle bed at three in the morning it is to dream of vaults of stones, boxes of jewels, people dancing in necklaces of rubies. I sleep at last in the moonlight decked in a robber's finery while those who populate my dreams glitter like Christmas trees and the golden heart locket lies against my ribs, warm as a kind hand. In my sleeping fancies I float through the sky on a magic carpet of my old bedroom door, now bucketless and exposed to view that night for the first time. The door was locked, the key in the keyhole, but I did not go in. I left that for another day because to go in there would be like looking inside my own ribcage, examining the contents of my own stomach and I will need to be rested for that task.

In the morning it is the truck from the City Council that awakens me much later than usual, the truck with Wallace's food. I have usually been up for a couple of hours before it arrives. Crates of lettuces today, a box of oranges, a large container of bananas, buns from the bakery, several loaves of bread, fruit and nuts, and the rest of the truck's tray taken up with a load of soft green cuttings from trees. Elephants prefer to pick their own but Wallace has been very tame for a long time. He may have been tame always, born in the circus or a zoo and encouraged as a bun-eater since earliest infancy. In the preceding weeks we have sorted out a good place for Wallace's daily deliveries of fodder, the truck driver and I, and I tumble down the stairs in my crumpled tunic to help him. My ears are still starred with ruby clusters, matching rings on my fingers, a knot of rubies round a wrist, diamonds kept solely for the blazing left hand and the golden heart tinkling on my chest.

"Just take these inside and put them somewhere safe," says the driver and plonks the cartons of buns in my jewelled arms, "while I unload the greens behind the shed." He is unconscious of grandeur, has no idea of what constitutes a jewel so my packing and unpacking of the treasure trove will remain a secret till it hits the auction rooms. "Are you rehearsing for a play or something?" he asked the first time I came out on to the front porch to greet him and I imagine, perhaps wrongly, that he will think I merely look a bit more tinsel-tacky than usual, a pantomime jade who has slept in her costume after *Aladdin and His Magic Lamp*. There is a nice shady spot behind the car shed where we have laid a web of pieces of timber, a kind of lattice to hold the daily load of fruit and vegetables slightly off the ground so the air can circulate, so Wallace can dine with his food in the best order possible. Please note my use of the word 'nice' and add that to my list of personal crimes. Apart from being too literary I may also be too nice in a sullied kind of way and that, in Hillingdon, constitutes an invitation to predation as well as being a synonym for 'fool'. We unload the lettuces and the fruit, a box of carrots at the bottom of the load, the last item unseen like some kind of vegetable riddle.

"Aha," says the driver, munificent in black overalls, insignia on the left pocket, "I wondered where they were. They were meant to go to the monkeys. Never mind. You can have them." Wallace has begun to breakfast on bananas and I pass him a bun or two from a selection I have put in a little basket slung over one wrist. The handle wrestles for space with a pearl amulet and more rubies, squarecut and set in platinum. Wallace's trunk roves over the load and he declines carrots. Possibly lunch, not breakfast. He takes another bun or two from me and stares reflectively into the distance, towards the house and the upper windows of the landing where I sleep. Behind those casements are my own jewels, my own secret store of bullion in the golden coat with its medallions and runes, a necklace of rare Burmese rubies, the sapphire diadem the maharanee gave me, my own diamonds and pearls, my matching bracelets, the jewelled tunics and shoes, all my banking system and unused as yet, the documentation for accounts in Swiss banks untouched in the lining of my Indian portmanteau. Like a much younger and cleaner Miss Haversham, written differently so she has a positive and not a negative view, I have cleaned the dust away from the corners, opened the windows, arranged the dispossession of the objects so there is more of my literariness for you. I have re-written *Great Expectations* for Charles Dickens and my surrogate child is an elephant, not the beautiful and wayward Estella.

I have subsisted, since my return, on the proceeds of selling more ordinary things from the house as I have packed. I sold the kitchen table and chairs, a lot of stuff from the bedrooms, all the furniture from the old morning room, everything in the conservatory, three chairs from the entrance hall, most of the china from the kitchen cupboards, everything utilitarian I could lay my hands on. I sold all that a month ago and that cheque from the auction rooms has kept me going till now. There has been no need to make discreet little trips to town, looking for signs on jeweller's windows saying "We Buy Gold." No need for that.

"I must say," said Goldblatt the week before last, "you've got a very neat figure, Margaret. A very, very neat figure, if I may say so. Now Muriel has a bit of trouble with all that. They're a big family, the Prendergasts. The women in particular are all very big." He sketches a few wild and enormous half circles in the air to denote, possibly, buttocks and breasts or, for the innocent, huge elbows and knees. "Oddly the men in the family are smaller. Her father was only five foot three. At the moment Muriel's on the Pritikin Diet. It's very new and she's lost quite a bit of weight but, sadly, she seems to have plateaued."

"I beg your pardon?" This terminology is beyond me.

"She's stopped losing at the moment. She's plateaued, Margaret. Plateaued. She's weighed the same for three weeks. She's getting quite desperate actually. I found her crying yesterday. Perhaps, Margaret?" he stopped there.

"Yes?" I said.

"It's a bit difficult, really." Goldblatt swished his big handkerchief over his bigger forehead. "Would you mind telling me what you eat, Margaret, and then I can tell Muriel. It might help her. Margaret, there's no need to laugh like that. Ssssh, Margaret. They'll hear you." He glanced through the inner windows to the typing pool.

"Goldie," I said, "if I told you what I eat you'd have a fit."

"Well, come on, Margaret. Tell me. Let me decide whether I'm going to have a fit or not."

"I eat bananas."

"Yes?" He is writing all this down. "What else."

"I eat lettuces and oranges and apples. And sometimes I eat carrots and nuts." That delivery man from the council often gets the monkeys' food mixed up with Wallace's, but I do not elucidate on this subject to Goldblatt. "I also eat about four buns a day."

"Buns?" Goldblatt has stopped writing. "What do you mean, Margaret, buns?"

"I mean buns, buns like you eat. You know the sort of thing, baker's buns, sometimes plain, sometimes with sultanas." It depends what is brought up to the house from the zoo. "Sometimes spicy buns."

"What about, say, eggs, Margaret? Or chicken?"

"Never any of those," I said. "Just, really, what you might call salad ingredients. And buns. Don't forget the buns. Sometimes bread, but not always. It just depends." Depends on the deliveries.

"Extraordinary. I must tell Muriel. What about cheese?"

"No cheese. But I do take iron pills because there's really no protein. You're supposed to have protein, but I'm taking the iron pills instead of eating meat." Perhaps if they brought me a lion, as well as Wallace, I could be a carnivore and gnaw goat steaks as darkness fell each night, chew on a horse chop at luncheon-time and give tiny barbecues just for myself with indefinable pieces of meat blazing over the coals.

"Does this diet have a name?" Goldblatt had wanted to know. "Is there a book? Perhaps Muriel could buy it."

It was a bit difficult, but I managed to get away with being unspecific.

129

"It's just something I've formulated," I said as I was leaving.

"Over the years?" Goldblatt was still writing.

"No, just recently, as a matter of fact. It's just something I do. I don't really think about it." The door of his office was already closing behind me. I wondered what Goldblatt would think if he knew I ate the elephant's food. If he did he would probably laugh at me and say I was more eccentric than ever he had supposed and that is the cruelty in such beliefs. I am only surviving as best I can. The peculiarity has come only by ill chance and it is not due to a fault or a wish on my part.

It is more than twenty years since I did any cooking and I am too busy packing up Mother's things to learn at this stage, so I share the food with the elephant. It has been good for me. I look extraordinarily well. It is all the raw food, I think, coupled with a little carbohydrate in the buns plus the iron pills to fill the protein gap.

After the truck has left, Wallace and I picnic gently under the trees and behind the car shed. We breakfast daintily, and very late, on bananas and more buns and then I leave him tethered to a lanky old rose bush on the eastern lawn that is now a wilderness. He will spend what remains of the morning picking apples from the top of the biggest tree and may rest, standing up, before a light lunch. It is time for me, though, to get out the old fountain pen, to find some less yellowed sheets of writing paper and formulate a message for Captain Kothari because his sudden and unexpected *yours very very sincerely* has haunted me for days.

Dear — and I stop then, the pen faltering to a halt in the kitchen where I always write, the mummified nose of a mouse skeleton forever peeping out from behind a piece of corner skirting board. What can I call him? His own letter gives me a map upon which to pin my own words. *Dear Miss Margaret Harris.* That is what he called me. My full name. So I pick up the pen again, heartened, and start to write.

Dear Captain Gulab Kothari, It was very kind of you to write to me and I very much enjoyed receiving the message because I miss my life in India and I miss everything I ever saw there and all the people I knew. I miss everything. When your letter arrived I put it on the mantelpiece and I spent all that day going back to look at it and read it again because it seemed, to me, that it was like a miracle. I have thought since then of the many times you drove me places or went on outings, and how you were always in the background or in the distance, and I wish now that I had spoken to you more. But I was too shy to do so, and I thought you did not like me.

If you are in contact with your cousin will you please thank him, on my behalf, for his very kind action in bringing my father's car back to this house? It was a long time ago, twenty years, but I am very grateful. I feel certain, from what you have said in your letter, that your cousin must have been the benefactor in this matter. Also, if you see Netta and Gopal will you please tell them that I miss them very greatly? I remember the morning we left, you and I in the big silver Austin, and I looked behind just once and was so pained I could not do so again. They were walking towards the City Palace. They had been sent from there originally, all those years ago, and I suppose it was natural for them to return. I hope they are well and happy, also yourself. I hope you are all well and happy.

As for me — well, I am in great trouble here. My mother and father's property, and the entire estate, is in a state of disarray but I am sorting it out. I have a problem with a neighbour who seems to be a very unpleasant man. He has claimed a building on part of the land, also some of the land itself and has already felled several of my large trees for firewood and has it stacked up at the back of his house, a most galling sight for me. This Saturday, only three days away, he says he is coming on to my land again to stake his claim finally to everything he says is his, and which is not, and I am not sure what to do.

After writing all this I sit for a long time staring into space. It is not fair to burden Captain Kothari with my problems yet I have no one else to tell my news to. Unrepentant, I continue to scribble.

He looks a mean man with a short thin upper lip stretched over a mouth that is grudging and rude. If that holy man from Agra saw him he would say that he was a man who gave out negative influences that would, in time, destroy him but I am not sure this will occur by Saturday. The City Council has given me a small elephant, on loan, to guard the property and he is my only solace and my sole friend in this place. If it were not for the elephant, Wallace I call him because they did not even wait long enough to tell me his name the day they delivered him, I would be in extremis *indeed.*

Anyway, it isn't fair of me to tell you all this because you are far away and have many things to do. Indeed, your own life may have many sad problems attached to it and to have the news of someone else's, loaded on to you, may be a crushing blow. If it is, do, please, accept my apologies. It is just that it is so lonely here and I am thought so little of. I realise now that I became very spoilt living in your beautiful city because I was treated with respect always, and people thought me lovely. I became spoilt, and have now become suddenly unspoilt and frightened. With very kindest regards and sincerest thanks for your kind remembrance, Margaret Louisa Harris. I give him the gift of my second name.

When I walk out the gate later in the day to post this message I find another piece of mail from India in the letter box, blank this time with no word upon it except for my name and address inscribed in dark ink, the capitals flowing and the lower-case letters as tiny as a careful thought. It is a postcard, brilliant as a jewel. The picture shows a room in a maharaja's palace, portraits of gilded and ornamented princes hanging in formations up the walls as far as the ceiling, the walls themselves covered in bottle-green brocade as rich and verdant as the better kind of cricket pitch. My father would have liked it because it would have reminded him of mowed lawn. I am not sure what he would have thought of the embossed scrolls and arabesques. Possibly he would have dismissed them from his sight and mind, as he dismissed everything he disliked or did not understand. The name of the palace is printed at the bottom of the card but it is not one I ever knew or visited and it is in a state far away from where I lived, a princely domain to the south and it may be where the maharanee came from originally.

As I hold the card in one of my glittering hands — I am still wearing Mother's rings and some of my own — I wonder if the maharanee has not, after all, taken up residence in the bungalow within the grounds of a palace on the edge of the desert. Perhaps she has gone home, just as I have.

The chamber on the postcard is empty of people. Grandeur is such that it could hardly be called an ordinary room. The picture shows no living soul but many who are probably now dead are pictured in their finery round the walls. There is not much furniture. An ebonised chiffonier or two, banded in thuyawood and with porcelain plaques on the doors, loiter against the walls, upper pediments tottering under the weight of ormolu and the later excesses and excrescences of the French Empire style. In the middle of the room a large round table in heavily carved dark wood looms, a matching set of four monumental chairs ranged about it, their liver-coloured marble seats discouraging any occupancy and, indeed, there is none. There is no sign anyone ever sat on them. A cushion or a person would have struck such a discordant note in this scene of empty and comfortless splendour that the picture would have been ruined, though the photographer would have had to be present, possibly just for a second or two. Above it all shines a green crystal chandelier with four prism-studded branches, all of them enormous and the whole thing is almost exactly the same as the one in the maharanee's sitting-room, the one we sprayed with the aerosol cleaner.

There is no message and any tidings, like a living person in the picture, would be superfluous. The maharanee has sent me this, I do believe that. And she wants to tell me that she is lonely, that her days are empty, that in the rooms she moves through there is not a friend, that there is no comfort or respite anywhere and the grand and empty room with the ranks of cold dead faces on the walls is like her life now. It is a gilded desolation. I, standing beside my mother's letter box and glittering with jewels, know now that we are exactly the same. My state is mirrored in hers. This despatch is about the silence of her mind, the emptiness of her heart and the fruitlessness of her womb and, wordless, it sits eloquently in my hands like the touch of a confederate or a sister.

Late that night I sit cross-legged in the entrance hall again. In front of me is the last bucket of jewellery to be sorted and boxed, categorised and valued. And I also have a selection of cards I have bought. From these I must choose one for the maharanee. Her whereabouts flicker mysteriously in my mind like the thoughts and memories I have when I lie in the moonlight on my truckle bed upstairs. Left leg outstretched, right leg bent and with the foot against the other knee, arms above my head, I recline like a toppled ballerina, a flesh-and-blood version of the dancer in the emerald and peridot brooch I have claimed as mine. Usually my thoughts are of my father's voice and the professor's damning final remark. *Please, Margaret, please. Don't be a nuisance.* There is, too, that other final echo of twenty years ago.

I don't really see, Margaret, how you found the time for all this, how you equated a balance between work and recreational activities such as, possibly, a healthy interest in tennis, like Sylvia. If you had balanced your time correctly, if you had had, for instance, a proper timetable, this would never have happened. There is an imbalance somewhere and I merely wish to draw it to your attention. Margaret, there's no need to cry like that, this is a rational discussion between hopefully rational people, in the very vain hope that such a thing might never happen again. I have your best interests at heart and although I'm speaking harshly, do believe me when I say I'm simply doing so for the best. If you had been more like Sylvia you would never have got into this terrible predicament. Nurse, I wonder if you could do something with my daughter? She seems to be hysterical.

I might also be dead because Sylvia is dead and, according to my father, everything she did was always correct. There are other telling little harping thoughts like that recollection of the goldsmith from the market. 'Madam' he called me as he worked amongst shavings of gold as bright as the flecks in the holy man's eyes when he said, "Sing to me, dreamer," so I knew it was time to go. It was like feeling the first hint of autumn in the air. Those thoughts are replaced now by the maharanee and where she might be.

The postcard showing a reception room of the unknown palace might have been the only one she could find of such a place. There were no cards ever marketed with photographs of the old City Palace I knew from a distance so well and close-up only once. She may, after all, have taken up her life of retirement in the bungalow nearby. The title went side-ways, to a nephew or a cousin — the maharanee was as childless as I was — and I wonder now, will she be called 'aunt' and thus be reminded again and again of her innocent fall from grace and power? Or she may really have gone southward, to her own family, to live. So the address is doubtful, and so are the cards I have bought.

Will I send her the one taken from a heraldic painting which shows a winged cupid sitting on a cloud all alone? His expression is tragic but serene and, behind him, the sky is black with an approaching storm. Too romantic and idealised. Or what about the one with a reproduction from a watercolour of an empty bowl, a shard of broken blue china to the left? Too gloomy and tragic. In the end it is the terrace I choose. There is a card showing a terrace bright with red geraniums, a pretty iron table to one side and an empty chair facing a view of the sea. A newspaper lies, carelessly thrown down, on the flagstones beside the chair. No person is present. Whoever was there has now gone, fled on some other business or perhaps summoned by bad news, but the terrace has charm and promise of a comfortable return because the chair is exquisite and the newspaper may be only half-read. The flowers are beautiful and the sky serene. Out of emptiness may come tranquillity, from journeys there could be glad returns. That is what I want to tell her, but I do not believe it myself as midnight strikes again. Midnight and I are friends and conspirators now. Again I greet the strike of twelve with filthy hands blackened by newsprint from the old newspapers I use for wrapping, a soiled tunic, muslin trousers baggy with kneeling before packing cases, hair disordered and tied up with a piece of old ribbon, but magnificently jewelled amidst the dirt like a beggar who has donned the contents of a parcel of precious things found in a gutter.

With the best fountain pen, newly filled with black ink, I inscribe the maharanee's address and nothing else. The Dowager Maharanee, The City Palace, I write, the rest of the words trembling in doubt upon the envelope. Even my block capitals take on a tentative air as I write them. Perhaps, if she is not at the bungalow, some official or another will send it on to her wherever she has gone.

Today I posted the letter to Captain Kothari and tomorrow I will post the card to the maharanee. Today the clerk said, "To India?" when I passed the letter over the post office counter for stamping. "To India?" In Hillingdon, perhaps, there are not many letters posted to India. Tomorrow it will have to be said again and I have no doubt at all that this sudden postal blooming of mine, this splendour of letter and card, will not go unnoticed. In Hillingdon they are like that. The news of two letters to India on two consecutive days, posted at the chief post office by a jewelled and daintily distraught woman clad in peach-coloured chiffon, may even reach Goldblatt's ears within a week, if he ever returns from Sydney and Gloria Thorpy. Muriel, meanwhile, will be grazing hopefully on four sultana buns per day, plus lettuce, carrots, oranges and bananas, and may still be plateauing to a greater or lesser degree.

But it is time for the last bucket of Mother's investments and the contents tumble out with a noise I have come to recognise as gold upon gold, silver upon silver, the odd handful of Krugerrands thrown in for good measure and the attrition of diamond upon amethyst, pearl upon agate to enliven the search. When my father died, Goldblatt sent me a statement of account for the estate tabulating the worth of everything. It struck me then that there was very little actual cash in hand, very little in the way of investments, no stocks and shares, no money put into unit trusts or let out with lawyers on mortgages. There was the house and the furniture, and that was all. My mother must have salted away all excess funds into possessions. The value of all her shopping, then, would have been dispassionately entered on the balance sheet, untaxed and unassessed, as nil. Household contents. Personal clothing. Bric-a-brac. I wonder what they called it?

There is not a lot that is of interest in the last bucket. It is as if the house and everything in it, even the lunatic and ancient packing, know I am nearing the end. Mother's profligate assemblage of dedicated shopping is a show that is nearly off the road. It is like the final night of *The Mousetrap*, the last note at the ending of *South Pacific*. Best find of the night is a three-string choker in grey pearls, ungraduated, and with a clasp that may be tiny diamonds but I am more inclined towards white sapphires. There is something opaque and very nearly unattractive about them. There are some gold bangles in varying weights, all nine carat and one with a beaded coral Art Deco trim to give snake's eyes to a circlet for a wrist. I am not very enthusiastic about any of this, though, because there has been so much and it is late and I am very tired. My packed shoe boxes, tonight, have writing denoting the contents in a wandering hand, a weary hand that vacillates over spelling and I have to consult an old dictionary for the terminology for gems. 'Cabochon' is a word to trip the unwary at three o'clock in the morning so, in the end, I write only 'uncut' on one box to denote unfaceted gems and beads of garnet and amethyst, tiger's eye and bloodstone, jade and lapis lazuli. The diamond rings, this evening, have been small but pretty and the colour has been good, a clear bluish sparkle that will find favour, I hope, at the auction, but there has been nothing to gladden the heart of a *chère amie*, a literary strumpet such as I am, except a small gold locket which opens upon the portrait of a tiny baby, unidentified and unrecognised. It might have been me, or Sylvia, newborn and possessing the anonymity of the newly hatched. It could be anyone's infant, even mine, so I keep this gilded item crushed in my hand like a secret message from the past. *This is your child — look upon its face and wonder.* The voice is unknown and anonymous. Perhaps it is just the chime of memory, the pulse of my own mind.

My bedroom door is now completely exposed, but still I lack the courage to go in. Will it just be four walls, a shell, in which I once lived and grew like a little crustaceous thing that became a flawed golden fish and swam away? Or will it be intact and shrouded in filth like the rest of the house, nibbled by mice, excreted upon by stray birds who may have got through holes in the plaster ceiling and the floor covered with the myriad onyx baubles of fossilised rodent shit? In the shadows cast by the door's architrave I find a sword in a steel scabbard, the handle finely worked with metal inlays and the blade gleaming in the moonlight when I flourish it over the banisters. My recollection of the people I went to school with — like Barry Goldblatt and the plateauing Muriel — is as vague as my memory of some of the things in the house. But I do recall that this sword once hung down in the entrance hall and belonged, long before that, to my father's elder brother who was a naval officer and died young.

Once again, dirty and unkempt, I sleep in my clothes on the truckle bed, the last of the packing finally completed for the carrier and the sheathed sword propped up beside me like a crutch. I might be a warlike invalid or a cripple inclined to violence. The dreams take me through the remnants of the night again, and I fly along on the magic carpet of my bedroom door, this time with an unsheathed sword in my jewelled hand, my own mythical battle cry echoing through the house as I see that vision of Goldblatt at The Arsehole's front door, the envelope changing hands amidst oily laughter and something I remember he said as the car door slammed.

"And more where that came from." The subconscious will sometimes fling up recollections that have escaped a waking mind.

It is nearly time for the battle of the garden shed, the tournament of the trees, the fisticuffs for the firewood. It is almost time for all that.

Chapter Eight

"Margaret? is that you?" Goldblatt's voice, echoing over the line from Sydney, sounds yellow with satisfaction, glutenous with delight. He is exactly like a talking custard. "Don't say you're still in bed, Margaret." In the background I hear a faint titter. Someone else is in the room with Goldie.

"How can I still be in bed when the telephone's in Mother's pantry. As far as I know I sleep upstairs, not in the kitchen, but you might know better."

"No need to get shirty, Margaret. Only joking, my dear, only joking. Sorry to ring you so early but we've got a long day planned here and we're making an early start." In the background I hear a tap being turned on and the water splashes down into a bath already well-filled. Goldblatt is in a bathroom with someone.

"Pass me the soap, darling. No, not the blue, the pink. No, not that one, that other one by your left hand, the one in the basket. Yes, darling, that one." The voice is distant, nasal, and haughty. Gloria Thorpy is in the bath and Goldblatt is supplying her needs in every possible way. "And don't go 'Shhh' at me like that, darling, and waggle your fingers. I don't like it."

The splashing of water is not exactly beside the telephone and there are tiny sounds of exertion from Goldblatt, so this could mean he is reaching out, passing things. The bath must be a small distance away, perhaps a metre or so, an arm's length. There is suddenly the rattle of something heavy falling and I now know exactly what Goldblatt is doing. The naked Goldblatt is sitting on the lavatory, mercifully with the

139

lid down. He is using it as a chair and in standing up to pass Gloria her fancy soap the lid stuck to his bare bottom, then fell with a clatter. Gloria has a telephone beside her loo and her bathroom fittings are of imitation marble because the sound was louder but deeper and more mellow than that from falling plastic yet contained the peculiar cheapness and sharpness possessed by imitations. Definitely pseudo marble. And all these fittings, even the bathroom itself, are either pink or blue to match the soap. I am sure of that. I have not lived for twenty years in a land where the merest nuance, the faintest rustle, has the direst significance without learning that a properly and improperly trained librarian reads every-thing including sounds on the telephone.

"Sorry," says Goldblatt. "I was just interrupted for a moment. Now, where were we?"

"I don't know." It is very early in the morning and Goldblatt was correct when he accused me of being still asleep when the telephone rang. The effort of leaping out of the truckle bed and running downstairs fully clothed in yes-terday's grimy draperies, whilst still dreaming of India and my garden there, has left me dizzy.

"You sound quite breathless, Margaret."

"I was riding the exercycle." This is a lie, but it is unwise to let Goldblatt know too much, injudicious to let him know that the carrier came yesterday and took everything away so that in the depths of the night I hooted through the empty house with the old vacuum cleaner, swabbed the floors again with buckets of boiling water and disinfectant so strong the fumes might gas a regiment. Unwise for Goldblatt to know I did not go to bed till three in the morning and that Wallace and I had buns for supper in the moonlight at two thirty.

"Good God! Did your mother have an exercycle up there? Extraordinary, Margaret. Is there anything she didn't have?" More titters and splashing. Perhaps Gloria has raised her legs out of the bathwater and is making cycling movements. Goldblatt's voice sounds strained, as if he is sweating.

"Not a lot." I am a grim and charmless woman this morning.

"Anyway, Margaret, what I'm ringing about is this call you made to Daphne a day or so ago. According to this message I've received you say the neighbour who's been causing trouble over the trees is coming actually on to the property tomorrow, Margaret, tomorrow — am I right in this? — to claim the garden shed and thirty feet of your mother's land? Is that right?"

"Yes." More of the grim and charmless stuff.

"Margaret," Goldblatt is the essence of patience, the pinnacle of diplomacy. "Margaret, my dear, I can hardly believe this." There is the sound of coughing from Goldblatt, violent whoops as though he is choking back Dickensian laughter. I can hear faint movements. He might be making supplicatory or mock-threatening gestures towards Gloria, a ballet of body language to ensure that Gloria understands they are a couple and I am, merely, a nuisance. "Are you quite, quite sure you aren't imagining things? It'd be very understandable what with the strain you've been through, long journeys and so on, jet lag, the shock of your mother's death and all the rest of it." Goldblatt cannot bring himself to say that Ranji, the maharaja, is dead and that I have lived in India for two decades as a Hindu concubine in a stone house of some considerable magnificence.

"'All the rest of it'," I say. "What exactly do you mean by 'all the rest of it'?" It would be gratifying to have one's own horrors at least acknowledged. There is a lengthy silence broken by a sudden burst of grudging laughter from Goldblatt. Perhaps Gloria has tickled his toes. Perhaps he has idly stretched out a short, plump, pink leg and Gloria, well trained in the arts of pleasure, has licked his knees with a long, athletic, pink tongue.

"Sorry, Margaret, sorry. I didn't mean to laugh at you. It was something else."

"I'm sure it was."

"I don't like your tone, Margaret. I feel certain I've woken you up with this early call and I've already apologised for that. By the way, what sort of night did you have?" This strikes an echo in my mind. Surely it is an almost perfect, and accidental, quotation from *Martin Chuzzlewit*?

"Middling." It is a long time since I read Dickens, since I wrote my essays and quoted at length, but I think the old nurse, Mrs Gamp, said, "Middling," in reply to such a question. "Restless." I think she might have said that as well. And it is my turn to smile secretly at arcane personal jokes on the telephone, to display my own personal language of exclusivity and exclusion.

"Anyway," Goldblatt the orator, Goldblatt the lustful lavatory-seat-sitter is in full spate now just like the bathwater in that distant rosy chamber as Gloria turns the tap on again with one manipulative foot (conjecture on my part), "to return relentlessly to the subject, Margaret, with regard to this neighbour there's very little I can do. I find it impossible to believe that anyone would contemplate the action you described so graphically to Daphne because it's entirely against the law and insane as well, as any child of five could tell you. It is positively bizarre. I can't believe that anyone, even a madman, would behave like that. When I get back to the office next Monday I'll write to him again, a more stiffly worded note this time, and we'll see if that does the trick." Goldblatt's ponderous utterances are Dickensian but lack, in real life, the charm they might have on paper.

"It won't." I am interrupting Goldblatt now. "And if you won't do any more than that, if you won't help me — and this is the very last day I've got to marshall any help because he's coming tomorrow, Goldblatt, tomorrow, and that means in the morning — I'm going to telephone Muriel and tell her where you are. I'm going to tell her you're staying with Gloria Thorpy, in Sydney." I add the location as if that, somehow, makes it worse.

A long silence, hefty and magnificent, descends on my mother's house and also on the distant bathroom. Even Gloria has stopped making dainty splashing noises, though she may have one, or even two, large coin-sized nipples raised above the water (more conjecture).

"I can hardly believe what I'm hearing here, Margaret, and I'm going to ignore it. I feel your whole attitude has become warped due to strain, and as an old schoolfriend I can only endeavour to view this with toleration and understanding. As you very well know I'm a very happily married man, a very, very happily married man, I can state this quite categorically with all truth, with three beautiful children and a very creative wife who was née Prendergast, Margaret, don't forget that, and don't ever forget that née Prendergast counts for something in Hillingdon. Do not forget either, not for one instant, that that very creative wife is quite a force in local business what with her venture into making concrete teddy bears and similar items for the better type of garden. And don't let it slip your mind, either, that you yourself are closely related to the Prendergasts, on your mother's side." This is the way people who are born in Hillingdon talk.

"Nevertheless, I'm definitely going to telephone Muriel straight away and tell her you're staying with Gloria Thorpy in Sydney." I have lived away from Hillingdon for a long time.

"You wouldn't do that."

"I would. And I'm going to tell her that you're in the bathroom, which is either pink or blue imitation marble with soap to match, and possibly towels as well, and you've been sitting on the lavatory seat naked, talking to me on the bathroom phone. Furthermore," and here I am carried away by my own eloquence and lack of power, "I can tell you I have the gravest suspicions of you in the matter because I saw you one night down at his place, down at The Arsehole's house, talking to him at the door as friendly as you like. And I saw you give him an envelope."

"It was a lawyer's letter warning him off." Goldblatt's voice is wary, though, very wary.

"Why not send it through the post? And, anyway, I'm still going to tell Muriel."

"You wouldn't, Margaret."

"I would." Twenty years is a lengthy period to be absent. "And I heard what you said. You said, 'And more where that came from.'"

"I did not."

"You did so."

"Muriel isn't home." Goldblatt's voice is chilly. "She's gone to a three-day live-in course at the polytechnic called 'The Song of the Shirt: Domestic Technology and Housework in the Twentieth Century.' You won't be able to get hold of her. They're not allowed to use the phone."

"I'll walk down the road and leave a note for her at Reception then. The polytechnic's not far from here. I'll tell the receptionist she must make sure Mrs Muriel Goldblatt gets it because it's urgent." More silence passes. "And it is."

"Is what, Margaret?"

"Is urgent, Goldblatt."

"Margaret, you'd be enough to drive anyone crazy. I'll see what I can do, and that's all I can promise." Goldblatt's breathing has become laboured. Possibly this has been caused by delight at the sight of the frolicsome Gloria mingled with horror at the thought of Muriel finding out about those frolics. "I'll give Daphne another tinkle. We've got a man we use sometimes at the office, a sort of trouble-shooter who helps out in the dirtier divorces or if there's a fight between siblings over wills and legacies, that sort of thing. Sometimes the going gets a bit rough even in the nicest families and even in dear old Hillingdon. Perhaps I could give Daphne a call and see if she could get him to keep an eye on the place for you. What time did you say the neighbour's coming in to claim the garden shed? If, in fact, he does?" Goldblatt's titter is filled with its own humour. I do not echo it. "As far as I recall, Margaret, your mother's garden shed was hardly likely to attract World War Three." Goldblatt is convulsed and in the background there is a faint tinkling, like that of ice cubes on crystal. Possibly Goldblatt and Gloria have been drinking Buck's Fizz as an early-morning celebration and Gloria has decided to pour herself another glass.

"Is this man big?" My voice suddenly sounds frail. I am very frightened and what has frightened me most of all is that my terror is considered ridiculous. "Because the neighbour's very big, and so is his father. He's bringing his father in as well, he said so. And there's a brother involved, too, so it's hopeless calling the police because he's engaged to the sister of one of the constables so they all think the light of day shines out of his Godamn ass." Americans used to occasionally visit my garden in India, but only when the roses were in full bloom and exclusively by appointment and for a fee. "And if it comes to some kind of confrontation about who's got the best ass and the best light shining out of it I aim to be the Godamn winner any day of the week."

"Margaret." Goldblatt is very faint and far away now. "Margaret, you've entirely taken the wind out of my sails. Please try to remember that your father was a very respected man in the town, once the president of Rotary no less. I'd never have thought that the cultivated and charming girl I went to school with, she who became that international figure of graciousness and charm we all know so well, would ever use language like that. I can't believe what I'm hearing here."

"Nor can I." This is the first sincere remark I have made today. "Do believe me when I say 'Nor can I.' It's a sign of how afraid I am, how menaced I've become, that I'd ever speak like this. I have become, sadly, noisy and profane and the worst thing about it, Goldie, is that I'm unrepentant, entirely unrepentant, and to hell with Rotary and all the rest of you. So if you won't help me I'm getting in touch with Muriel to tell her what you've been doing."

There is another very loud rattle from the lavatory seat. Goldblatt is standing up now, straight and tall for the execution.

"I'll ring the office straight away, Margaret. I'll get this chap on to it for you, and that's all I can do for the moment. But please — and I do implore you — don't ring Muriel or leave a message for her at the polytechnic. We've got Grandma to consider — her heart's far from good — and next Tuesday the landscape architects are coming in again to recast the back garden in the Italian style. I simply can't face a tremendous upheaval in the house with the garden all dug up, Margaret, I really can't. There'll be piles of earth everywhere. It's going to kill me, and that's before I even get the bill. I implore you, as an old schoolfriend, please reconsider your stance on this. The marble statue of Minerva, in profile, weighs at least a tonne and there are all the flagstones to consider as well as the actual soil. We're having three large truckloads of top soil brought in for the continental *parterres*." There is another lull in the conversation and small sounds of exertion from Goldblatt. He may be washing Gloria's back, or front. "And don't forget, Margaret, you still haven't signed

145

that thing for me. One good turn deserves another. I'll expect you to do so with some alacrity when I return. Now what time shall I tell Colin Fosdyke to go up to your place?" Only Goldblatt would have a security guard with the surname 'Fosdyke', I think.

"I don't know what time The Arsehole's coming in," I say. Goldblatt's garden is of no interest to me and the idea of possibly being rescued by someone called Colin Fosdyke lacks a little lustre. "I can't give you a time," but the telephone at Goldblatt's end of the line is already clattering on to the cradle and a gigantic splash ends the conversation. Goldblatt has jumped into the bath with Gloria (conjecture again).

The sun is beginning to slant into Mother's pristine pantry now and I hear the truck from the botanical gardens start its slow journey up the pitted drive to the house. Our breakfast, Wallace's and mine, has arrived. Also lunch and dinner, possibly supper as well with the balance of the buns eaten in the moonlight amidst the falling dew and autumn leaves. Winter is slowly coming down upon Hillingdon. The telephone begins to ring again and Goldblatt's voice is already pouring forth as I lift the receiver.

"So sorry, Margaret, I've made a mistake, my dear. I forgot, Colin Fosdyke retired last week. Only fifty-seven, a tragedy really, but he had a long-standing knee injury and it didn't respond to treatment so he took early retirement with a lump-sum package our accountant worked out. We had a bit of golden handshake drill down at the office and a little party for him. Muriel arranged it all. She's marvellous in a crisis. The chap who's taken over is a bit younger — I'd put him around fifty-two, fifty-three, somewhere round there. Bert Wayne's his name. Watch out for someone called Bert Wayne. He's a skinny little bugger, pale blue eyes, going bald, rather a shiny red face and he seems to have trouble with his feet, though he's assured us it won't interfere with the job. Our accountant's one of those bloody awful New Wave Christians and he was very keen to give him a chance, though I must say I wasn't remotely impressed. It seems he has some kind of unfortunate history, I don't know what, but he's on trial for three months, and that's all I can say. I thought I'd better tell you or you'd be waiting for Colin and you wouldn't know who Bert was. Oh, yes, and about the feet. I don't know quite what's the matter with them but he takes his shoes and socks off and sits barefoot in the sun airing his toes at the drop of a hat. Something to do with the circulation, as I understand it. Diabetes, or some such thing. A bit off-putting, but you don't have to ask him into the house. Anyway, I'll leave it with you, Margaret." Another splash ends this addendum to the main conversation. Goldie is back in the bath.

In the night I awaken and walk through Mother's empty house in the moonlight. All her shopping, everything of every size and description, has been in the auction rooms for more than twenty-four hours. The place is now very clean. All signs of residency by droves of rodents have gone. The smell of disinfectant and yellow soap that has been my sole shopping at the supermarket is piercing and soothing, the rooms like wards in a plague hospital awaiting patients. Down in the auction mart the furniture and cartons, the boxes and crates, the jewel caskets and shoe boxes full of necklaces, rings, brooches and bracelets, real and otherwise, may even be numbered already and cataloguing could have begun on Hillingdon's most definitive estate sale to cause teacups and much else to rattle throughout the town. Possibly even beyond it.

Outside, Wallace has wandered out on to the seaward lawn and I watch from an upstairs casement as he stands like a dark deity or a myth I might have imagined in the remnants of my father's garden. In profile against the brightness of the moonlit sea he looks like an elephant I once saw in a sixteenth century embroidery. The coloured silks and the careful cross-stitch showed a melancholy pachyderm immured forever amongst English game birds and wildflowers in medallions upon each corner, the face of the animal, in silhouette, *distrait* against an ancient ocean. I love Wallace but it is time he went back to the circus where he belongs because I have little to offer him here except a brief sanctuary, as brief as my own, and trouble and pain and aggression and spite, gossip and unkindness. For we have not been accepted by the people, not at all. I love him, but he needs more.

"Just give them time," Goldblatt always says. "Had any invitations lately? Had any invitations at all? None? A pity. Never mind, Margaret, just give them a bit of time and they'll come to accept you. It's just a matter of waiting. Sooner or later they'll realise that you're really a very nice person at heart and underneath all that," he waves a hand at my tunic and draperies, my pearls and my gold, "there's still the same old Margaret they all went to school with. Perhaps next year or the year after you'll look back on all this and laugh, Margaret, because by then you might have made a little circle of friends. You might have got to know one or two people. I must say, and I mention this for your ears only, I was very disappointed that Raewyn stood you up like that. I would've thought better of Raewyn. She's usually a very caring person, or so we all thought." Another of those long silences elapses, the silences I have come to know so well. "The McTavishes breed Great Danes," says Goldblatt.

"I don't like dogs. I don't want a Great Dane."

"That's not what I mean, Margaret. You've missed the point entirely. What I mean is the McTavishes breed Great Danes and Great Danes are rather a large dog, Great Danes are an enormous dog, not to put too fine a point on it. Great Danes are not all that much smaller than that bloody great thing you've got up in the garden, and if you added up the weight of all the Great Danes the McTavishes have got in their kennels they'd probably weigh about as much as your — well, you know what."

"You mean my elephant?" Goldblatt is treating Wallace as if he is a figment of the imagination, a distortion my fever of fear has produced.

"Your elephant, Margaret, if you must dot every 'i' and cross every 't'."

That is how Goldblatt goes on and I have grown very tired of it.

"Gerry McTavish went to school with my younger brother Des." Goldblatt is still wittering on. "They were in the fourth form when I was in the sixth and you were, I think, in the fifth. Correct me if I'm wrong there. And Gerry's wife, Liz was née Liz Smith. Her father was old Smith who started up the big television shop down in the middle of town when television was just the newest thing since sliced cheese — you probably won't remember that, probably you'd gone by then — but the old boy made a fortune out of it, a fortune. Liz was an only child and inherited a mint of money when Smithy-Boy kicked the bucket, and now she's gone deeply into dogs. She was always rather a doggy sort of girl. Perhaps Liz might be a nice friend for you to have, Margaret, as you're both so fond of animals. She had a younger sister called — oh, God, what was that girl's name? — but she was more what you'd call a horsey sort of girl. I don't know where she lives now. I did hear she married some chap called Flannagan, or was it Finnigan, who had a racing stable, but whether he was a trainer or a jockey or not I don't really know and as far as I can remember, they lived up Auckland way, just south of the motorway and off the main road in some big spread with a silver birch avenue and the fences all whitewashed." Goldblatt runs on at great length on all occasions.

But I am suddenly tired of it all. It would not be possible to wait for a year or two before I had a friend here because I might die of loneliness before then. And I have a feeling of finality. The furniture and clothes, the jewels and the hats and shoes dating back to the 1920s have all gone now. The mess is cleaned up. The dirt is a memory. I have used up most of the soap, all the disinfectant, the scrubbing brushes are worn down, the broom is broken. The girls on the check-out at the supermarket have ceased to stare at me because I have become a familiar sight and they are programmed into the idea now that I buy only soap and disinfectant and brooms and brushes.

"Don't you ever buy food?" one of them asked me once.

"No," I said, "I get it given to me." I was wearing a pale apricot sari that day and her eyes suddenly contained a dawning and erroneous understanding that I was a Hare Krishna.

The rodents are dead and the birds have flown away. Even the old roses down in the garden have been jerked into life by liberal applications of elephant shit, depending on which way Wallace has been facing. Everything is different now. There is only my old bedroom to face, plus the battle of the garden shed, and then it will be time to go. Prawar Bros will be sending for Wallace very soon and I cannot remain here without my only friend. The holy man from Agra used to say that time and time again men will find a new heaven, and I feel it is time for me to look for mine.

At three o'clock in the morning with Wallace, surreal as a dream, standing guard outside my windows, I place my hand upon the big brass key in the lock of my old bedroom. Three in the morning is a peculiarly anonymous time of night, an hour of fancies and nightmares when a wakeful sleepwalker can view the horrors and magic of her other lives. Some dreams, I have read in reference books, take only a few seconds and yet encompass everything in the subconscious. I cannot bear to look inside my bedroom officially, by light of day, so I filter in as if I am dreaming, soft as a moonbeam, as the clock strikes three.

The first thing that strikes me as being very interesting is that the key turns easily in the lock, and when I pass my hand over the brass fittings I sense a film of oil that is quite new. Mother died last September, nearly six months ago, and this oiling of the lock would date from then. All the other locks in the house were clogged with rust, keys concreted in position by dust and decay, when I opened rooms filled with Mother's packing with its population of mice, dead and alive. But here, at the entrance to my old room, everything is oiled and nearly pristine. The wooden door feels as if it has been waxed and there is a faint scent of lavender that becomes more marked as I push the door open in the moonlight.

There are blue and white china bowls on the floor, filled with dried herbs and pot-pourri and at the windows hang bunches of dried flowers. Rosemary for remembrance swings here, tied with pink satin ribbon, the elaborate bows with four loops each and the ends of the ribbon trimmed into neat vees. Someone went to a lot of trouble with this room. And there are no packing cases, no crates, not a box in sight except

150

a huge old camphor chest with brass bindings and carrying handles that would once have been a trunk to take on board a ship. When I open the lid I find, neatly piled and wrapped in new tissue paper, my old jerseys, my overcoat, the clothes I left behind so long ago. The silk shirts are also wrapped in tissue, the nightdresses folded neatly in four. The furniture is covered with dust sheets and when I pull them away everything is as I left it. My oak bed with the slat ends stands against the outer wall, just as it always did, and it is made up. It is ready for immediate occupancy. The sheets are fine old white linen, the pillowcases encrusted with pale embroidery. Everything is white, as if for a bride or an innocent child. The blankets are of fine snowy wool with satin bindings and my mother must have bought them especially because I see their price tickets dangling, the dockets of recent date, so she must have worked on this room not long before she died. My dressing table is still there with its oval three-wing mirrors and the doilies of fine ecru tatting, the reflection of myself in triplicate, blanched with sorrow, for at last I have begun to cry for my poor mad mother. Amongst the silver-topped bottles and jars of new cosmetics she must have bought for me, lipstick in a pale bronze and eye pencils of smokey grey kohl, the largest-size bottle of Chanel No 5, the essence not the toilet water, there is a note propped up against a vase of dried roses.

My darling child, I hope one day you will return and find all the things I have bought for y— . I cannot read any more.

Early in the morning the flickering of a tiny light, like a star, on the ceiling of my bedroom awakens me. This little ray glimmers amongst the plaster swags and festoons like the sun's reflection off water, but there is no pond in the side garden any more, no puddle to catch the first light. I dreamt of cemetaries, in the remnants of the night, graves in orderly rows, flowers beneath neatly chiselled headstones. The faint odour of mustiness, the feel of a room that has been shut up for months, has filtered into my nostrils from the white linen sheets. A moth or two fluttered out as I slid into my old bed and death must have been on my mind as I fell asleep. But it

151

is tailored and ordinary death, with the usual accoutrements, of which I have dreamt, not funeral pyres nor the wailing of a multitude, and now with the little light shining on the ceiling I lie there only faintly curious about what has caused the glitter. Perhaps the reflected light is from dew on the tops of flowering trees, or from a tiny water-hole I have not yet discovered beneath the weeds. Child-like, and rested at last, I lie within the safe cocoon of the pretty bed my mother made up for me. There are other charming little pinpoints of light to cast prisms upon the walls and those come from the beginning of the sun's daily slant on to the crystal bottles, still polished, and the silver mirror and brushes on the dressing table.

I remember that morning very well and I had a lot to look at as I lay there, in my old bedroom, and just for an instant or two I had a feeling of happiness and safety, an ultimate luxury. It was then, at that exact instant of security at last, that I heard the murmur of voices from below. Someone was down in the trees that stretched along the forested boundary, more than one person was down there, and when I looked out of the window I saw exactly that the pinpoint of light that winked and glittered on the ceiling of my bedroom came from the sun's reflection on the blade of The Arsehole's chainsaw. It was swinging from his right hand like a spidery supplementary limb as he stood talking to an older man, possibly his father, and there was a third person walking down the buttock of Mother's garden marking the trunks of trees with slashes of chalk. Possibly the ex-All Black who was engaged to one of the constables. From where I stood at the little upstairs window I could see the beginning of a numbering pattern. 1, 2, 3, 4. They were establishing a programme for the felling. The Arsehole had arrived to take over the land.

CHAPTER NINE

SO THERE THEY are at last, those three figures on my dark hillside. They are like exclamation marks within a dramatic narrative exploring a deed most foul and, like a fourth mythological figure in the telling of a drama, I grasp the naval sword as I go downstairs towards the doors of the old conservatory. Beyond the innocence of my mother's unsaleable and tattered seagrass chairs, past the windows of coloured glass lie the grove of trees and the land The Arsehole covets as well as the garden shed with its stout door that swings in the breeze since he broke the lock. On the seat of one of Mother's battered old chairs lies a letter I received yesterday and I read it again before I go outside. If there were another person in the house I would clasp that person's hand for an idea of strength and warmth but there is no one here, so I re-read the letter. It slipped into the letterbox yesterday in a long slim envelope, thin as a whisp, pale as the baby's cheeks pictured in the locket I wear now against my heart, as small as an infant's long-fingered hand.

Dear Miss Harris, You will not know me but I am writing on the instructions of my cousin Gulab who says he knew you in India. We have received a letter from Gulab today telling us that he plans to visit this country. He instructed us to let you know immediately and he said to tell you he would be writing to you as quickly as possible, probably later in the week, when he has been to Delhi to make his bookings. He wanted to be able to tell you exactly when he will be arriving and in the meantime wanted us to let you know this news. It seems he has notched up many years of work and has not taken the required holidays so he is going to spend some time trav-

elling. We are all looking forward to seeing him. We have never met but we all have a great affection for the idea of our family. My father, who is now ninety years old, is making great plans about the visit. He sends his apologies to you, Miss Harris. As head of the family he felt he should write to you himself, but his health is not good. Last year he had a stroke which affected the use of his hands and he hardly ever, these days, takes pen to paper.

Once again I am deeply enmeshed in Indian hierachies. I know there would have been much talk about the correctness of everything, the proper form of it all and whether it would be best for the head of the family to write to me or to allow his son to do so because the son's hands are not paralysed and he has probably written notes, on matters of business, to many strangers in the course of his lifetime. And I also now know that, apart from having a cousin here, Gulab has an old uncle.

I would like to shout that I am terrified of The Arsehole and he is in my garden trying to steal parts of it at this very moment. I would like to shout this so loudly that Gulab Kothari's cousin would hear me hundreds of miles away in the seaport I once drove to around three sides of a geographical square the night the legendary storm altered the country forever. I stand there quietly though, shrugging my shoulders in Mother's isolated house in which I am so far from the road that no one would hear me if I called out for a week. Goldblatt has said so and he would know. Possibly he has tested the accoustics.

There is the sound of paper rustling now, so I know my hands are trembling.

I have begun to draw the sword from its scabbard and I tuck the letter against one of my cheeks, hold it there with one hunched shoulder. I imagine that it is like a hand held against my face, the comforting touch of someone I may love. The garden is still silent, graceful in its withdrawal for the moment, but The Arsehole will surely begin soon.

Do believe me when I tell you that I'm very grateful for your letter. How very kind of you to write. It's so lonely here. Did Captain Kothari really write to you and ask you to enquire about me? Really, really and truly? And is he really coming to see me soon?

When your letter arrived I cried with such joy, and laughed at the same time, that you would not believe that anyone could make such a noise. Already, in my own mind, I am writing my own reply.

Our cousin was most lyrical about the beautiful Miss Margaret Harris and her safety and happiness. The cousin's note ends with this magical phrase, and when I read it again I begin to bloom like a brave late flower. The garden remains hushed, the chainsaw mute. I listen carefully with the letter propped against my cheek, the sword in my hand.

With the great blade unsheathed I went out of the conservatory doors and down the old concrete stairs to the garden, my muslin and chiffon draperies flowing after me like a tide, diamonds blazing on my left shoulder. I walked tall and straight and true, like a knight emboldened and illuminated by love, for I knew then that my mother had loved me in her own odd way and that there were people in the world who loved me even if they were far away. The dead walked with me, not in any ghostly way because I do not believe any of that, but they marched with me, in love and solicitude, within the invisible memorabilia of my own mind. I remembered my mother, when I was a little girl and before everything went wrong, how she held my hand in hers when we crossed the road.

"Always look to the left, then look to the right, darling," she used to say, "then look to the left again, just to make sure, before you cross. Now, you will remember that, won't you, little wunchy?" And I remembered my father, my poor dry father, with one of my reports in his hand. I might have been in Standard Two or Standard Three.

"Very good," he said, ebullient words from him.

And there was Ranji. I heard him bounding up the stairs when I arrived in my pink house at last and he was shouting, "Where is she? Where is she?" with such laughter in his voice that I laughed as well. And I cried, too, so when he saw me all the careful work, the kohl round the eyes, the hair piled so beautifully and held by a golden circlet, it was all ruined by tears and laughter.

"Sing to me, dreamer," the holy man from Agra had said, so I walked with the sound of old songs echoing in my ears.

Within my own spirit they all walked with me as I went down through the garden with my sword. Garlanded by yearning and devotion I held the blade in my right hand and I strode straight up to The Arsehole as if I walked with an army.

"Get off my land," I said and I put the point of the sword under his chin where it just broke the skin, nothing more, and I watched while the beads of blood formed and trickled down his neck like a veil. "Get off my land and don't come back." For a moment I took the sword away and swung it in a wide circle. The blade cut the cardboard label that was hanging on the end of a piece of string tied to the chainsaw's handle and it also neatly sliced the knees off the trousers worn by the older man, The Arsehole's father.

The cloth flew upwards, like two autumn leaves and the garden was full of those that day. His knees, shining through the holes, looked suddenly like two astonished eyes.

I think I should clearly state here that at no time in this exchange was Wallace present. He was round the front of the house peacefully eating apples. There were three apple trees in the old garden, varying species unknown to me. Wallace was very fond of apples and he had gradually stripped the trees. The apples he was eating that particular morning were from the third, and last, tree — a smallish fruit with a striped skin, possibly a 'Cox's Orange' but my knowledge of such matters is limited. At no time was Wallace anywhere near and he cannot be held accountable for any violence. It was all my doing. I was alone, apart from my thoughts. Wallace was waiting round the front of the house for the man to come with the food. Animals can judge time very accurately and nothing would have budged him from the front of the house then.

I looked into The Arsehole's eyes and I saw the beginnings of doubt and fear forming so I swept the sword in another arc and held it under his chin again so it broke the skin in another place, nearer the throat this time. There were two fine shallow slashes now and two veils of red dripping slowly down to his shirt collar. The man with the chalk was already climbing over the wire fence and the old man was turning back.

"Get off my land," I said again, the voice as soft as a whisper, fine as the wind. You can look into a man's eyes and know what he is thinking. The Arsehole's eyes were small and an indeterminate shade of hazel-grey, khaki eyes the colour of clay when a flood has passed. I knew that he would turn and run because I saw it in his eyes before he even moved, and after he had gone I stood on my hilltop, with my mythical army and my sword, listening to the silence that fell so sweetly over everything. A thrush began to sing far away down in the valley.

The Arsehole had dropped the chainsaw amongst the trees near the fence, so I went down through the shrubbery to get it and I heaved it over the fence into his own place. It began to roll, to bounce down the hillside, leap over the hollows in his garden. I watched it hit a big stone that edged his rockery and it flew up then in a wide arc, taken by the impetus of its own weight, and it went through The Arsehole's big plate glass window at the back of his house. The noise was like the breaking of a frozen sea. The bird stopped singing. After that I went back to my own house and I sat on the front steps in the sun, waiting for the police to come and get me.

The Arsehole was a vengeful man. He would call the police. I knew that. He would show them the cuts under his chin, the blood dripping down his clothes, the damage to his house, the chainsaw lying like a canonball inside the broken window, its passage down his garden marked in the broken soil like the scars he would have one day upon his own flesh where I had cut it twice with my sword till his blood ran. So I sat in the sun and waited for them to come and get me, and when Wallace handed me a bun I ate it because I had not had any breakfast. The affray had made me hungry.

They arrived much sooner than I expected. I gave The Arsehole ten minutes to run inside, to clap a towel to his throat, tell the tale to his wife, to re-tell it to his father and the other man while they said, "Yes, yes, that's how it was. And isn't she ugly. Wasn't she vicious." And then they might have walked outside again, staying in the safety of their own garden now, and shouting up through the trees, "Bloody rich woman in your great big bloody house," like The Arsehole and his father had done so many times before. I gave them ten minutes for all that, to give them time to let the gorgeous idea of my arrest, my imprisonment, my deportation perhaps, to bloom and grow in their minds. "We must ring the police." I allowed ten minutes for all that, but the police car appeared at my gates and came nosing up the old drive, through the weeds and the sow thistle that was going to seed, when I had only just taken my first bite from the bun. It would not have been more than two or three minutes since I turned from the sound of the shattering glass and went back to the house. It was still quite early in the morning and the sun had reached the front steps where I sat down. This is a lie. I sank down on to them because I could go no further, yet I felt very happy in a blanched and terrified way because I knew The Arsehole and his friends would never return, that I had cleared the land and cleaned the house. I had a feeling of completion and accomplishment, and when the car stopped I just said, "Hello," as casual as you like to the man who wound the window down to look at me. I remember I thought it was odd that there was only one of them. Usually you see two policemen together in those patrol cars.

"Miss Margaret Harris?" he said. "Of 25 Hillingdon Avenue, sole beneficiary in the estate of one Ivy Evelyn Harris, formerly of this address?" I took another bite of the bun, because I was hungry, and I didn't say anything. What I thought was that if I were to be taken away then to the police station I might never return to the sun and the warmth and the sound of the birds in the old trees. I wanted to savour it.

"I'm looking for a Miss Margaret Harris." He was having another go at it, climbing out of the car as he spoke and I also remember I thought it unusual that he was wearing a suit, an ordinary business suit with a striped shirt and a silk tie. I had expected a couple of constables in full uniform, with caps on, and perhaps they might have sent that stupid girl again, that one who suggested I needed counselling because I objected to The Arsehole stealing my trees. They might have sent her again. I had already thought that as I made my way back to the house.

"Could you tell me where I might find her, please?" he said. "I've been told she lives here but," and he was sizing me up now in my muslin and chiffon Indian tunic and those trousers they wear in the north, trousers rather like soft jodphurs in silk or chiffon and falling in folds at the ankles, "perhaps she doesn't. Perhaps you could tell me where she might be." I stood up then because I had finished the bun and it was also time to begin dealing with it all.

"I'm Margaret Harris. Do you want me to come down to the police station?" I picked up the sword that was lying on the steps and the tip of the blade was red with fresh blood. "And shall I bring this?" The holy man once told me that silence is a clear message. I decided to remain as silent as possible and, thus, they would all slowly learn of my recalcitrance, my violence under provocation, my obdurate will that no living soul would be allowed to steal my land and my property. Others may have babbled of the battle, sworn an innocence or a provocation, but I thought of the holy man and said nothing.

"Interesting piece," said the man in the suit and he took the sword from me for a moment, felt the weight of it in his hands. "A most interesting piece. You've got a very nice cutlass blade there. Probably it was a naval officer's sword, nineteenth century I'd say." He had given it back to me by then and I saw that the blood was drying, browning in the bright sun. "I'm a bit of a collector," he said, "but I haven't got anything as good as that. Could I ask where you got it from?"

"It was always just in the house. When I was a child it used to be propped up in a corner of the entrance hall. No one took any notice of it. My father used to say it had belonged to his brother. He was in the navy. He was a lieutenant in the navy. If it's a very old sword might he have bought an antique one? Or been issued with one? He died quite young, before I was born. I don't know much about him." So together we stood in the sun and inspected the sword again. The blood was going even browner by then. There was still no noise or outcry from The Arsehole's house.

"Most interesting," he said. "I could waste a lot of time up here. It's rather beautiful." He looked round the garden as if he loved it — perhaps he was a man who had an interest in land — and Wallace gave me another bun.

"I heard you had an elephant up here," he said and he went over and patted Wallace on the front left knee as if he were a tall horse. "Good boy," he said. "Will he be all right if I do take you down to the station? We won't be very long. Half an hour should do it. It's just that I've got all the files down there. It'd be more convenient, really, for both of us, if I could talk to you down there. I tried to ring a bit earlier but there was no answer."

I just said, "Of course. I was probably out in the garden. I've been trying to clean the place up before it's put on the market. And are you quite sure I won't need this? No?" So I went inside the house for a moment and propped the sword up inside the front door. So they had files about me at the police station, I thought.

"Do you need a handbag or anything?" He seemed a pleasant man. "There's no hurry. You can take your time." He had come to the front door and was staring into the emptiness of the front hall.

"My mother lived here for quite a long time by herself," I said. "The place got into a bit of a mess. She wasn't very well. I've been cleaning it up. I lived in India for many years but I came back here," and I did not use the word 'home', "three months ago." He might have thought the emptiness, the reek of disinfectant, was unusual. Most houses are furnished and lived in. My mother's house had, for many years, been in an increasingly unusual state and the fact that it was now empty and clean made it no less unconventional.

"My wife's in Little Theatre. They're doing a kind of shortened version of *The Pirates of Penzance* at the moment, just a few of the songs. It's more what you'd call a concert but they like to call it a show." He had wandered into the house now. "You've got some very fine leadlights there." He was pointing to the windows beside the old fireplace in the sitting-room, but he was looking at me. "I thought you might be in a play or something. I was trying to think who might be putting on *Ali Baba and the Forty Thieves*," and he nodded at my clothes, "but I realise now, of course, from what you've said, that you're the lady we've all heard about, the one that came back from India. It was that elephant — the elephant reminded me. Of course, of course. I've got you placed now. Have you got everything? Don't need a handbag or anything? A jacket?"

So I ran upstairs and got my golden jacket with its magic runes and discs.

"The station's a bit draughty, so they say," he said when I returned. "They've given me an office on the sunny side, but as I won't be here after next week it's all OK by me. I'll have finished by then." I stood there thinking he seemed young to be retiring. "Are you sure that blazer's going to be warm enough? It looks very thin." I just nodded, dizzy by then with my own pretence.

"Now, are you certain we won't need this?" I said again as we went out the front door, lingering for a moment beside the sword. I gave him his chance. "And should I pack a little bag?"

"A little bag?" he said. "What for?"

You can't say I didn't give him a chance. I thought they might keep me down at the station in the cells, that I might need a toothbrush and another tunic, more jewelled shoes, my jewel case. But I climbed into the car with him and he suddenly said, "Oh, you haven't seen this," and he passed me an ID card. He was a detective inspector from Wellington, in the Fraud Squad, not even a local man, so I sat in silence all the way into town because I believed my crime must be a serious one to deserve such attention and my own peace and stillness might be my only protection. They would say it was abuse, even though I had not said anything much to The Arsehole, with menaces or battery and violence, even attempted murder. I remember very vividly that I sat in the police car worrying about Wallace all the way down to the station, what would happen to Wallace if they kept me overnight in the cells.

When we drove out the gate the detective inspector said, "Just look at that house down there. They've got a very badly broken window. If it rains before Monday they'll be in a spot of trouble, won't they? Not easy to get someone to mend a big window like that at a weekend," and I just said, "Yes." Just plain and dour I was, like a stone talking. We went the rest of the way in silence.

"Do you know this man?" he asked me when we were settled in his little office. It was mounded with files and he took some off a chair so I could sit down. He handed me a photograph from a folder but I kept it face down because The Arsehole's mean face with its short upper lip pulled tight over big teeth, the small clay-coloured eyes, was something I wished to forget. "Can you identify this man?" he asked again and gestured at the picture. He might have been irritable or perhaps he might have been in a hurry with other people to see. I understand that now.

"I do wish you'd have let me bring the sword, and a bag." I had begun to tremble by then, I suppose it was the fright of it all. By now the blood on the blade would look dark brown in the dimness of the hall, like dirt that gathered over the passage of years.

"Look," he said, and he leaned forward so I saw that his eyes were a bright warm blue, "if you're worrying about the sword, don't. According to the Arms Act 1956 any householder can possess an antique piece of that kind. It's guns that are the problem. You'd need a licence for a gun but there's no problem at all with a sword, I do promise you that." He leaned back in his chair. "As a matter of fact," he said, "I'd be interested in offering you a good price for it myself if you were interested in selling. I've got a bit of a collection, as I've already said, and that's a very fine piece, that little item you've got up there."

"Oh," I said. The word was as round as a pear ripening on a tree.

"But we can talk about that later," he said. "If you'd just have a look at the picture and tell me who it is I'd be really grateful. It's been a long haul but we might be able to nail him now."

"But that's Goldblatt," I said when I turned the photograph over. I had kept it face down on my lap. "That's Barry Goldblatt, my mother's lawyer. He's married to Muriel Goldblatt who's got some business or another manufacturing concrete teddy bears for people's gardens. I was at school with them years ago. Muriel was Muriel Prendergast before she married Barry. I was in the fourth form when she was in the sixth form but if you talk to her she'll tell you it was the other way round — women are so mean to each other about how old they are, aren't they? And Barry Goldblatt's father was a butcher years ago. He was the one who put up that yellow building up on the hill that's all let out as offices. Goldblatt's got his own office there on the third floor. What on earth do you want to know for?"

"And may I ask you to look at this photograph, please, and tell me who this person might be?" I might not have spoken. He took no notice of my question.

"Good God," I said, "that's Gloria Thorpy." The supine figure of the long-legged Gloria was shown reclining in a hammock strung between two palm trees on a tropical beach. Beside her, on a small carved table, was a martini shaker and two glasses, both full. "She's a tart in King's Cross, very high class. I went to school with her as well. She was always like that. She was always very tall and had those long legs. When we were both in the fifth form she didn't pass any exams but she got a huge silver cup at the school prize-giving for being freestyle champion at the swimming sports. I was in the same form as Gloria but she never spoke to me, or not that I recall, because she thought I was a boring girl, a boring pill of a girl who wanted to be a librarian." I waited for a while then. It sometimes takes many years for these resentments and admittances to surface. "And I was," I said.

"Was what?" The detective inspector stopped writing and seemed to be waiting.

"Was boring and a pill and a librarian."

"Oh, I see," he said. He was ruffling through various sheets of paper. "I've only got one more question and then you can go home. I'll take you back myself if you can wait for a minute or two. Now, what I have to ask you is this, have you signed anything lately in Mr Goldblatt's office? Has he asked you to sign a piece of paper? It would be power of attorney to give him jurisdiction over your funds, over your mother's estate. Have you signed anything like that?"

"No," I said. "I couldn't find my glasses. I think I must have packed them up by mistake in one of the boxes and they're down at the auction rooms somewhere. I told Goldblatt quite clearly lots of times that I wouldn't sign anything unless I'd read it. My father was a lawyer and that's what he used to say, that you should never sign anything until you'd read it thoroughly, possibly even overnight in your own home. That's what he used to say."

"Thank you, Pops." He seemed an ironical man, the detective inspector.

"And besides," I said, "he really annoyed me nagging and nagging on like that. I just made up my mind I wouldn't sign anything even if he shot me. I thought he was a real arsehole." I must have had the word on the brain.

You know the rest. You know all about the headlines in the papers. SHOCK ARREST OF CITY LAWYER. MULTI-MILLION DOLLAR EMBEZZLEMENT SCANDAL BREAKS. BLONDE FLEES SCENE AFTER BATHROOM DEBACLE: TWO CONSTABLES TO FACE MOLESTATION CHARGES. HER BODY WAS SO ENTICING, SAYS POLICEMAN AFTER GUILTY VERDICT — I AM NOT SORRY. ONLY ONE CLIENT ESCAPES FLEECING. WILY HINDU REFUSES TO TALK. FORTUNE INTACT, SAYS POLICE SPOKESMAN FOR PRINCESS-LIBRARIAN. SECRETARY AND STAFF CONFESS: WE DID IT FOR LOVE. LAWYER AND HAREM, STORY INSIDE ON PAGE THREE.

You know all about that, and you would have seen the photographs in the newspapers and on the television news — a wilted and puffy Goldblatt peering out from under a hood as he was bundled on to an aeroplane to return home; leggy Gloria, clad in a designer négligé, speaking delicately of alleged ravishment whilst reclining in a hospital bed, her hair looking magnificent; Muriel slamming the front door of Chateau Goldblatt, the brief glimpse showing her oddly deflated, like a scone left out in the rain; a shot of me taking Wallace for a last walk round the garden. It was a special occasion and I dressed for it in my golden jacket, the maharanee's diadem and a pair of trousers in cloth-of-gold with anklets of matching diamond-rimmed coins. We had less than one more day to spend on the property.

I had to take Wallace down to the railway station to put him on the train the following morning at dawn. That was all the sudden message from Prawar Bros had said, relayed to me via the police station's fax machine and delivered by the detective inspector who came up to the house again to collect the sword. It was too late to send it down to the auction rooms and I was tired of packing. We agreed on a suitable price and he took it away to add to his arms collection. The holy man used to say that one must wait patiently for what time brings, but in the case of my attempted murder of The Arsehole — and that is an exaggeration because I wanted him off the property and that is all — time very quickly ensured that the evidence was hidden in a place nobody would think of looking.

"The blade seems a bit dirty," I said when I gave the detective inspector the sword, and he merely replied, "I'll give it a clean when I get home. They come up a treat with a bit of Brasso on a soft cloth." It was very low-key.

I must say Wallace came out extremely well in all the photographs. I stand beside him holding a rope so thin it looks pathetic, my eyes as dark as pansies, chiffon draperies ruffling in the breeze and the golden discs on my jacket looking as innocent as pennies or buttons. ANIMAL-LOVING HINDU HEIRESS INSPECTS ESTATE. ANIMAL-LOVING HINDU PRINCESS-LIBRARIAN REFUSES SIX-FIGURE SUM FOR LIFE STORY. HINDU ROYAL ANIMAL-LOVER GOES INTO HIDING. I found it very interesting that in the space of a day or so I graduated from being a wily Hindu to peripheral royalty, scholarly as well. It's funny how the media takes a fancy to someone sometimes.

The last headline is completely untrue. I did not go into hiding. I am not in hiding. There was nobody to help me take Wallace down to the railway station at dawn on that Sunday morning, less than twenty-four hours after I had nearly cut The Arsehole's throat twice, so I set off by myself. I was used to handling the elephant. It was not difficult and there was no traffic at that hour of the morning, none at all. I don't think we saw a living creature, except for a cat on a gatepost, all the way down into town and across the main street to the railway station opposite the library. The curtains there had been changed again, I noticed. Wallace walked along behind me and even though I held the rope, just out of courtesy to him, there was no need to. He would have gone with me any-where. I was very upset that I had to part with him, and I had one of those headaches you get when you've cried a lot, one of those dull bruising aches that you can't get rid of and no pill will lift, as if you've been hit on the head with a blunt piece of wood. The stationmaster came out when he saw us coming along the street. I walked in the middle of the road, I don't know why. It seemed easier than going on the pave-ment, which was pitted and narrow, and there was no traffic, none at all.

"If you stay at this end of the platform," the stationmaster said, "you'll be right in front of the truck it's supposed to go in. You've got three minutes to get it loaded after the train pulls in, that's all. Don't say I didn't warn you."

"He," I said. "His name is Wallace." I sounded like a mother defending a child, naming it clearly so all would know it was hers. All those years ago I should have stood on that pavement, dragged myself upright beside a parking meter and stated just as clearly, "This is mine. Her name is —" And I should have thought swiftly of the most beautiful name in the world. I should have done that then so now I said, "His name is Wallace," so a statement of claim could echo down the years. But the stationmaster had gone, back into his office, just as the crowd had dispersed countless years ago and the ambulance driver might have died of old age by now.

There was only one photographer out at that hour of the morning. I saw no one except the stationmaster, but someone must have been there because I have since seen a series of pic-tures of the train leaving. First of all there is a shot of me in my golden coat and my diadem and I am saluting Wallace, or so it seems. Actually I put my hand up to my face because I felt so sad. Then there is a second picture of the train arriving and Wallace and I are forever captured in the moment of action when we both begin to walk towards his truck. Wallace looms, gloomy and magnificent, against the mists of Hillingdon, and I am veiled by now because I drew a drapery over my face to hide my malaise. There is a third picture where we are both at the open side of the truck, at the beginning of a steel ramp that leads into it. Inside, if you have a magnifying glass of any strength, you will be able to see a sack of carrots and a few bales of hay. Then there is the magic picture of Wallace turning towards me and lifting me above his head with his trunk as he walks into the truck, and the last picture shows me sitting on his back as the train leaves the station, the face of Wallace serene and confident and my own filled with sudden joy, my draperies flowing in the wind.

I have never returned to Hillingdon. The final sight I had of it was as the train went slowly out of the station and, gathering speed, breasted the big hill on the edge of town where the ten-acre blocks begin and men like Goldblatt live in a state of magnificence with splintery reproduction furniture and wives who smell of perfume too expensive and too liberally applied too early in the morning to thighs and arms dimpled with cellulite. That is the last I saw of the place.

We went away from Hillingdon, Wallace and I, in the silence of a Sunday morning with The Arsehole everlastingly mute on the subject of his bullying encroachment and equally silent about the shameful battle he had lost as much on Goldblatt's behalf as his own, both motivated by greed and both failed. The cuts on his throat would have healed quickly because they were shallow and clean. Goldblatt was probably at that exact moment being arrested or might have been sitting in a cell already, earlier search warrants having been taken out on his offices and house so they had been fully explored. In one of the earlier newspaper stories about Goldblatt's case, the curious phrase "causing undue influence to be borne by clients who may have been elderly, ill or vulnerable in some way" was used, and this assemblage of words could describe exactly that little tableau I saw of Goldblatt and The Arsehole laughing at The Arsehole's back door. That large flat white envelope changed hands and The Arsehole, turning, gave a gluttonous last smile. Goldblatt drove away quick as a shark in his silver Mercedes while The Arsehole flapped the envelope as a goodbye gesture like the movement of a carrion bird's wing, bleached by its own deceit and rapacity. But Wallace and I journeyed swiftly away from that place for the train was picking up speed and the very last thing I saw was the sun finally coming up over the sea. Even then it showed signs of being a really beautiful day.

THE EPILOGUE

You could come and see me if you like, and bring all your children. Do bring the children. If the circus visits your town within the next two or three weeks you could find me in the dark blue caravan, with the powder-blue pennant flying from the television aerial, second from the left inside the main gates. If you get lost it's the one with the big basket of toys beside the steps. There may be children playing there already because some of the people in the circus have families, but I've bought plenty of toys and there are more inside. The caravans are always parked in the same way, regardless of where the circus performs. Mr Prawar likes it that way because it's easier to find people for rehearsals. My mother would be extremely pleased because in the two weeks since Wallace and I left Hillingdon we have both improved markedly. We have worked up, as Mother would say. I feel Mother would be pleased. Wallace had got a bit slack with one or two of his routines, but a few rehearsals set all that right. They were not sure about me — understandably so — but Wallace would not perform without me so I had to stay, at least until he had settled in again.

For the first two or three performances they put me in a special costume, a kind of sparkly pair of very brief togs, and all I did was stand by the big red velvet curtain and curtsy and gesture to the various animals or performers coming out into the ring for their acts. I used to have the spotlight on me, briefly, for the announcements but there was always deafening applause and such a lot of flowers and fanmail I graduated dramatically by the end of the week. Mr Prawar was delighted with the burgeoning crowds.

So I've been promoted now and if you don't want to come and say hello to me at my caravan you could all wave to me during the performance. ANIMAL-LOVING HINDU PRINCESS TAKES TO THE HIGH LIFE. You might have seen the latest stories in the newspapers. For the first two nights I was put into the trapeze act I just stood about twenty feet up the rope ladder and took up a ballet-type pose when the trapeze artists — Violet and Rollo — per-

168

formed. I've always had a very good head for heights, of every sort. But it was very boring doing that so then I was allowed up to the first platform to stand there, but only at the back; Violet and Rollo are the stars and I am only the helper, to hold the swings. I swing them out at appointed times and after particular signals. It's a matter of timing and it's very important to get it all exactly right or Violet and Rollo may fall. Wallace stands below, steadying the safety net, and in the grand finale we all climb down the rope ladder and on to his back into a kind of open carriage, thence beginning a parade, to tumultuous applause, round the ring. Rollo and Violet's costumes are more elaborate than mine: a darker blue with more and bigger sequins and the strapless top of Violet's has wings extending from it. My costume is plainer but cut very high at the thighs and low in the front. When Wallace carries us slowly round the ring at the end of the act I am the one standing at the back, the tall one with the golden hair. And my crown is real. Violet's tiara is only glass, but I wear the maharanee's diadem with the cabochon sapphires so you could recognise me by my jewels. Do wave and if you're sitting on the side of the Big Top opposite the orchestra I'll be able to hear you if you shout out, "Hello, Margaret." I'd be able to hear the smallest voice of the tiniest child, I would really. So don't forget to say, "Hello."

As for my mother's estate and the house, I have discovered it is possible to do anything. It is possible to telephone real estate agents from distant cities and authorise the sale of a property. It is possible to engage a packing firm to go to an unoccupied house and pack the few clothes left there, the odd flutter of chiffon and muslin, a leather case containing jewels, an Indian bag made from antique carpet with a few precious documents packed into the lining, the ornaments on a mantelpiece, the contents of a dressing table in a dormer bedroom, even a cherished note left thereupon. It is perfectly possible to do all that and it is also perfectly possible that these things will arrive safely where they are required. Nothing is impossible. Bottles of Chanel No 5 will arrive intact, also lipstick, eye pencils, anything. Lawyers horrified by the alleged misdemeanours of one of their profession will work indefatigably to wind up estates, to settle debts, to honour the obligations imposed by the sincere wills of strangers. It is also possible to do other things with just a signature on a document.

"Are you absolutely certain you wish to do this?" my new lawyer said last Tuesday. "Have you thought it through, Miss Harris?"

"Yes." My voice sounded like a cut of my sword the day of the battle for the garden shed, but there was no blood spilt, no fear of any sort. The only blood would be in the veins of children in places I might never see. There would be books for those who did not have them, places in schools, food for those who were hungry, kindly anonymous hands to deputise for mine on small shoulders and voices saying, "All come this way." In time a hundred children would become a thousand and then ten thousand. Some of them might become lawyers like my old father and he would be, anonymous and unknown, in their dusty prognostications. And when a child might be taken on a nurse's knee to be fed by hand, the hand would be like my mother's when she took mine and we crossed the road. We would all be there, even my sister Sylvia laughing in the twilight on the old swing we had in the apple tree. Sylvia would be there in new laughter. We would become, unknown to each other, a secret family of the lost and forlorn, the hungry and the hopeless and we would live better this time round. We would do better when we had another crack at it. There might, in time, even be a pianist.

"Are you absolutely certain?" said the lawyer again as I scrawled my big bold glad signature, the one Goldblatt always wanted and never got.

"Yes," I said as I gave him the pen he had lent me and, when he looked at me as if I might be mad, I said, "You'll have to understand that I'm an absurdly sentimental woman, just like my mother." I went away then, out of the office and into the street, because I had done everything I wanted to do and there was nothing more to say.

I have also written to Mukesh Kothari to tell him where I am and a slim letter in a navy-blue envelope addressed with golden ink by Captain Gulab Kothari has been sent on to me by the real estate agents who check the letter box every two or three days.

My dear Miss Margaret Louisa Harris, I was very much saddened to receive the news that you are lonely and in despair. Please try to remain cheerful because very soon I will be coming to see you. I hope by the time you receive this my cousin has also dropped you a line. I have many holidays owing to me so I am taking some time to travel. At the end of the month I will set off and will be in your country in a little over three weeks' time. Do be of good heart. Perhaps it would be a good thing if I told you a little about myself so you can think about these facts in the interim.

I own a stone house slightly smaller than your own in our very beautiful city but the agate inlays on the marble walls of the loggias are said to be very fine. My garden, alas, is a sad sight because I do not have much time to devote to its arrangement and my gardener is a lazy fellow who needs constant supervision. Perhaps if one day somebody else were here I could look forward to having roses of every kind. The new maharaja has disposed of various things including some of the cars in the fleet we knew so well, you and I. I have been fortunate enough to be able to purchase the silver Austin in which we set off on so many picnics. You may remember this. I now own the dear old Austin. Sadly, the new maharaja has not inherited his late Uncle's Ranji's passion for motorcars. When I stand looking at my motorcar, in my mind's eye I see the form of the lovely Miss Margaret Harris sitting in the back seat with one of her so very beautiful sunhats upon her golden head and once again we are setting off for one of those happy days in the countryside visiting historical ruins and picnicking in the shade of many a beautiful tree. I have the very definite idea that you once professed a preference for the Austin, so when it was time for me to make my choice there was not one to make. Fate made it for me.

As for other news, I think it would be best if we talked of things when I arrive, in exactly twenty days from this moment. I have the calendar before me now. I look forward very much to seeing you. Please try to keep in good spirits. My cousin Mukesh Kothari will contact you, as I have already said. I should tell you, I think, that I am a fully qualified accountant and I also have a law degree although I have never practised in that field. But we will speak more of these things when I arrive. Please, as I have already said, be of good heart because I will soon be there. Yours very, very sincerely, Gulab Kothari.

I've written back. I told him about the battle of the garden shed and everything that has happened and about his cousin Mukesh

Kothari writing me the kind letter, all that. And I explained about the circus, how I came to be at the circus. The letter should get there before he leaves. I've worked out that the turnaround for a letter to the north of India is two weeks. To be safe I've told Mukesh Kothari where I am and what town Prawar Bros will be in when the captain arrives. They're all going to make a special trip to see the performance on the eighth of next month, even the old father. In the meantime he's been making a scrapbook of all the newspaper clippings and the photographs.

It will be a fateful moment for me when I look down at Seat 1 Row A when we do our circuit of the ring on Wallace's back and I see, sitting there, neatly furled as an umbrella, the dark and enigmatic figure of Captain Gulab Kothari. I'm not sure what I'll think. Possibly I may remember what the holy man from Agra once said to me, that even the severed branch grows again and the sunken moon returns: wise men who ponder this are not troubled in adversity.